PENG
LIFE OVER ...

Sanjeev Sanyal is an economist, urban theorist and writer. He grew
up in Sikkim, Kolkata and Delhi before heading off to Oxford as a
Rhodes Scholar. He spent the tumultuous summer of 1993 in South
Africa as it transitioned from apartheid, and then extensively travelled
through Guatemala as it emerged from civil war. These experiences
made him a keen observer of rapidly changing societies, an interest
that reflects in many of his varied writings.

Sanjeev spent most of his adult life battling international financial
markets, a few years in Mumbai and many in Singapore. One day in
2008, mostly on a whim, he decided to move back to India and travel
all over the country with his family. This resulted in his hugely popular
second book, *Land of the Seven Rivers*. Then in 2011, again for no
particular reason, he went back to finance and took up a role as the
global strategist of one of the world's largest banks. He also spent the
next few years exploring the Indian Ocean rim—Oman, Sri Lanka,
Zanzibar, Vietnam, Indonesia, and up and down India's coastline.
These travels resulted in *The Ocean of Churn: How the Indian Ocean
Shaped Human History*.

Currently Sanjeev lives in New Delhi where he serves as the
principal economic adviser to the Indian government.

ADVANCE PRAISE FOR THE BOOK

'I have been a fan of Sanjeev's non-fiction books for long. But with *Life over Two Beers*, he has delivered a stellar book in the fiction space as well. A collection of short stories that are bitingly funny, and yet, deeply insightful of the many issues and conundrums that trouble our country today. Sanjeev, in this book, is like a combination of a wry Wodehousian author and a rebellious journalist taking on all the various elites that harass the Indian masses. Do read!'—Amish Tripathi

'Deliciously witty and irreverent stories that are cleverly crafted and force one to turn the page'—Ashwin Sanghi

'Sanjeev is one of the most illuminating and path-breaking writers of our time. His work on history has made waves again and again, and now his fiction is destined to do the same. This sparkling, acerbic fiction debut brings alive every contemporary issue and reveals new layers and complexities in them. There is no detail too small and no cut and thrust too obtuse for Sanjeev. He notices and unfurls them all. Impossible to put down. Delightful'—Hindol Sengupta

SANJEEV SANYAL

Life Over Two Beers

and Other Stories

PENGUIN BOOKS

An imprint of Penguin Random House

PENGUIN BOOKS

USA | Canada | UK | Ireland | Australia
New Zealand | India | South Africa | China

Penguin Books is part of the Penguin Random House group of companies
whose addresses can be found at global.penguinrandomhouse.com

Published by Penguin Random House India Pvt. Ltd
7th Floor, Infinity Tower C, DLF Cyber City,
Gurgaon 122 002, Haryana, India

Penguin
Random House
India

First published in Penguin Books by Penguin Random House India 2018

Copyright © Sanjeev Sanyal 2018
Illustrations by Jit Chowdhury

ISBN 9780143443292

Typeset in Aldine401 BT by Manipal Digital Systems, Manipal
Printed at Replika Press Pvt. Ltd, India

www.penguin.co.in

MIX
Paper from
responsible sources
FSC® C016779

To Shukra, for daring to see the world as it really is

Contents

The Used-Car Salesman

Rishi Taneja glanced out over the open terrace from the *barsati*, his new home. His suitcases stood in the corner, the British Airways luggage tags still sticking out like ears. The room was not large but it was well furnished with everything a bachelor might need, even a small television screwed on to the wall opposite the bed. There was a large doorway that opened on to a terrace and a stairwell that led down to the rest of the three-storey house. Rishi, now in his late thirties, had moved back to India after more than a decade in England.

He had grown up in the small, dusty town of Saharanpur. His father, a widower, owned a small shop in the bazaar selling hardware that just about paid the bills. Rishi, the only son, had shown no inclination to take over the family business. He just could not see himself spending the rest of his life stuck in a nondescript shop selling pipes and paint, sipping endless cups of milky tea and exchanging local gossip with the cloth merchant next door. He wanted to see the world, perhaps make a name for himself. However, Rishi's ambitions were not matched by any obvious skill or talent. He had been an indifferent student in an indifferent local college. He had spent his time watching Bollywood films and dreamed of becoming a famous star, but there seemed to be no door that led to any kind of stardom.

After failing to get a suitable job in one of the larger Indian cities, he managed to persuade his father to take a loan and fund him to go to the United Kingdom to study, a one-year course at a lesser-known institution near Reading. The content of the course was immaterial; it was just a ticket to freedom. A neighbour's son had taken the same route a few years earlier and now had a comfortable job in Manchester.

The year passed quickly and Rishi finished the course with middling grades. He even managed to get a clerical job in an insurance company in Cowley, Oxford. The job did not pay particularly well, but Rishi saved enough each month to send home money to pay back the loan. For a while it looked like his life was set on rails and it was only a matter of a few years before he gradually rose to office manager. Not quite the life in the spotlight that he had dreamed of, but at least it all looked certain. But two years into the job, things went awry. His father died of a sudden heart attack. Rishi returned home to Saharanpur for a few weeks. He sold off the old family home and the struggling hardware business, settled various debts, and went back to

Cowley. He had been promised a promotion within a year but, six months later, he was out of work, his role having been outsourced to Bengaluru.

Now thirty years old, Rishi was in many minds. He looked for jobs all over Britain, but struggled to even get interviews—wrong work visa, skill mismatch, recession and so on. He could have gone back to India, perhaps Bengaluru where his old job was now located. But he knew no one in the boom-town and did not relish having to start all over again. He thought of asking a distant cousin who had started a new software venture, but that would have been awkward, a last resort. Besides, he really knew nothing about software.

With his savings eroding quickly, the young man was reduced to doing odd jobs, from shop assistant to courier. It was after a tense year on the edge that he landed a job, quite by chance, at a boutique showroom for used luxury cars. It didn't sound like much, but it was here that Rishi discovered his true calling. Within six months he was selling as many used cars—Porsches, BMWs, Bentleys, Rolls-Royces, Ferraris—as his more experienced colleagues. He read up on the brands, their histories, picked up the nuances of different models. He keenly observed the customers who purchased these cars and learned how to impress them and earn their trust. It was not just the horsepower of the car but also the complete feeling of luxury for the upwardly mobile.

Soon a clipped upper-class English accent appeared, along with a couple of well-cut suits. Rishi learned to speak knowledgeably about expensive wines that he had never sipped. He visited the grand galleries in London so that he could casually refer to Monet and Manet.

It was a great act, and Rishi was soon a favourite with a certain fashionable set in Oxfordshire and their glamorous friends in London: hedge-fund manager Jeremy White, design consultant Javed 'Sammy' Isfahani, serial entrepreneur Peter Kowalski to name a few. They had country estates near Oxford and apartments in South Kensington. Rishi bought and sold them luxury cars as they climbed the social ladder. He was making a good living and rented a tiny but trendy apartment in North Oxford. A string of women drifted through his life. He also befriended a couple of research scholars at the university. He would drive them around the Cotswolds in expensive cars that he borrowed for the weekend, and soon he was invited to college dinners and punts on the Cherwell.

Five years passed in this way and Rishi would not have minded if it had gone on forever. He had never been so happy and content. But once again, fate intervened when the financial crisis ended the party. As markets crashed and corporate profits plunged, the hedge-fund manager took severe losses of his derivatives portfolio, the design consultant quietly went back to a Toyota Corolla and the serial entrepreneur sold his country estate and simply disappeared from the social circuit. There was suddenly a glut of second-hand luxury cars that no one wanted to buy. Rishi's employers drastically reduced staff to stabilize their business and even their star salesman had to be retrenched.

As if things were not bad enough, Rishi fell very ill and was bedridden off and on for several months. The NHS doctors were never quite sure of the cause and treated the symptoms till his persistent fever left him. As the recession intensified, there were no suitable jobs, and Rishi's savings were again dwindling rapidly. Physically, mentally and financially shattered, Rishi felt that the world had conspired against him. Sitting alone in his flat, with an intermittent fever, he felt trapped.

~

He was wondering what to do next with his life when he received an invitation to have dinner in London with his cousin Dilip Taneja, the software entrepreneur who had by now made it big. Dilip came from a more successful branch of the family that had included doctors and lawyers, and now boasted a software mogul. Despite the recession, Dilip had recently listed his company at record valuations. The cousins met on a sunny summer evening in the lobby of Dorchester

Hotel. They strolled over to the trendy restaurants at Shepherd's Market.

Rishi was not especially close to Dilip and had only met him on a few occasions before he had left India—family weddings and dinners. In recent years they had exchanged pleasantries on Facebook for important festivals and birthdays. Under normal circumstances Rishi would have been reluctant to ask Dilip for help. However, he was at his wits' end and he explained his situation to his cousin. Dilip heard him out patiently.

'I cannot offer you a job in my company as I keep business and personal relationships strictly separate. However, no brother of mine is going to starve if I can help it . . . so let me make you an offer. Come back to India, rebuild your health and restart your life. I have a fully furnished and staffed house in Delhi. It has a lovely barsati where you can stay as long as you like. You can use the rest of the house too. The staff will look after all your daily needs. Does that sound like a deal?'

'Very kind of you—thanks for the offer—I might take it up.'

'And, while you look for a job, you can also help me out. We are so busy between Bangalore and Silicon Valley these days, Vinita and I hardly visit Delhi. I have a bunch of real estate investments in and around Delhi—a farmhouse, an art gallery and so on. If you are willing to manage them for me, I would be happy to provide a generous stipend. What do you think?'

'Give me a couple of days to think about it. I will get back to you by the end of the week.'

By the time Rishi reached his apartment, he had already decided he would take up Dilip's offer. Delhi would be a new adventure. This is how he found himself one monsoon afternoon in a barsati in Delhi.

~

The new life was certainly very comfortable. Dilip's house was in a quiet lane in Hauz Khas. The house was done up in a corporate interior designer sort of way with lots of expensive art and large sofas. The middle-aged cook seemed glad to have someone to fuss over and Rishi's health recovered steadily from elaborate home-cooked meals. The problem was that he knew almost no one in Delhi. He also needed to find a proper job.

Rishi began to systematically inquire about jobs in and around Delhi. There seemed to be plenty of openings but they were mostly entry-level opportunities in media companies in Noida, or white-collar outsourcing factories in Gurgaon, suitable for a much younger person. Manager-level recruitment demanded prior experience or formal qualifications. Delhi can be a snobbish place, and degrees from lesser-known institutions and experience as a used-car salesman do not open doors.

Rishi tried to contact a few old friends from Saharanpur who had moved to Delhi. They met, they shared a few bottles of beer, talked about the old days. However, they now had their own lives and other concerns—wives, kids, jobs, pet peeves, mortgage payments, school admissions. The link of their childhood no longer held them together.

So it was that Rishi had a roof over his head but was adrift in a sprawling, buzzing city that had no time for him. To entertain himself, he took to walking over to Hauz Khas Village—the remnants of an old village engulfed decades ago by the city, now a warren of bars, fashionable restaurants and high-end boutiques. He wandered around the narrow, winding lanes and the adjoining medieval ruins. He browsed designer shops, chatted with bored Manipuri salesgirls, and made friends with a paan-seller who hailed from Saharanpur. When he had had enough, he would stroll across to the art gallery owned by Dilip's wife—one of the properties that he was supposed to keep an eye on.

The gallery was not much more than a large room. Abstract paintings hung sparsely along the wall. Like many such art galleries in Hauz Khas Village, this was a vanity project started by Dilip's wife and was not expected to make money. It was managed by a young curator who was happy to have company on quiet afternoons. She made a pot of tea and they chatted about this and that. On some Friday evenings, however, the gallery would be crowded for the opening of a new collection. There would be some wine and cheese, a press photographer or two, perhaps a speech.

It was at one of these events at the gallery that Rishi met Dolly Roy—mid forties, somewhat overweight, wearing faux tribal silver jewellery and the general air of a diva. He later learned that she was a literary critic of some standing. Her verdict on literary novels and poetry was considered the last word by the authors she promoted (but not by those whom she unsparingly critiqued). She always had a couple of aspiring litterateurs hovering around her, reiterating and echoing her views on everything under the sun. Of course, Rishi knew nothing about her when they first met.

'Dolly . . . Dolly Roy.'

'I am Rishi Taneja. Pleased to meet you.'

'Ah, the owner of the gallery, I presume.'

Rishi saw no reason to correct her. 'Hope you are enjoying the wine. I really think a Merlot would have gone better with the cheese, but I could only find a decent Pinot. Margaret River.'

'It's fine. It is so wonderful that a successful man like you supports culture . . . most Dilliwalas, you know, don't get culture . . .'

'One does one's bit.'

'So, I wanted to ask you if we can use the gallery for book readings . . . you know, writers and poets can introduce their new works. It would be so wonderful.'

'I am sure we can accommodate that once in a while . . . as long as it does not interfere with the Friday opening events and the artist on exhibition does not mind.'

'Why would they mind? My book readings bring in people, you know, the sort of people who appreciate art. But we cannot really pay . . . it would have to be gratis . . . Good publicity for your gallery though!'

'I am sure we can work something out.'

'Oh, it really is so wonderful that a successful entrepreneur like you supports culture.'

Dolly gave him a big hug and left with her entourage.

Dolly Roy got her book readings. They brought in a few dozen people for an hour, once a fortnight. The sales of paintings saw no change as the audience was mostly made up of retired civil servants and aspiring writers, none of whom could afford the prices. However, Rishi enjoyed the events. He met new people and played the role of a patron of literature. His clipped upper-class British accent became a little more pronounced, and he made references to Manet and Monet. The old civil servants nodded approvingly at his allusions to Oxford colleges and their arcane traditions. He listened attentively to their wise solutions to various national ills but had the good sense not to ask why they had not implemented these proposals during their long and illustrious careers.

It was only a matter of time before Dolly invited Rishi to attend one of the literature festivals that had sprouted all over the country. He was uncertain. It was one thing to occasionally play patron on his own terms and quite another to spend all day listening to authors he had no intention of reading. Indeed, he was finding the book readings at the gallery increasingly tedious. But he still did not have a job and decided to attend one of the larger events to see what the fuss was about.

The literature festival was held in a colonial-era 'palace' once owned by minor nobility, now a heritage hotel. Rishi arrived a little before noon. There were two parallel venues— one in the courtyard and one in the front lawns where an elaborate marquee and stage had been erected. The grounds also had stalls set up by publishers to hawk their books. A little beyond the ornamental fountains, there was a bar and some food kiosks. There were some chairs and tables under an open gazebo where people sat sipping coffee, engaged in animated conversation, soaking in the winter sun.

Having surveyed the grounds, Rishi drifted back to the courtyard where a session on poetry was under way. The venue was half filled. The session was moderated by a middle-aged TV anchor known more for a love of controversy than poetry. One of the panellists, Ashraf Mahmood, was recognized for his efforts to revive a nineteenth-century style of storytelling using Urdu rhyming couplets. The other was Sir Alistair Blackbourne, an old-school poet complete with silver hair and a somewhat worn tweed jacket patched on the elbows.

The former car salesman sat in the last row. He had acquired many skills during his years at Oxford, but an appreciation of poetry was not one of them. The discussion did not interest him, and he anxiously looked around for Dolly or some other familiar face: nothing. He fiddled with his phone, wondering what to do next when, almost by reflex, he googled Sir Alistair. As a young man in the sixties, he had been a minor member of the 'Chelsea Set' and had hung about Fantasie Cafe with Mary Quant and the beautiful people. He later became well known when Philip Larkin wrote a glowing review of his second collection of verse *The Deceived & the Garden*. He was knighted in 1998. Rishi followed links to some of his poetry including *Bleany's Garden*, written on Larkin's death.

The panel discussion ended and the floor was opened to questions from the audience. As is customary on such occasions, most of the time was used up by an ageing professor who delivered a monologue entirely unconnected to the preceding discussion. The audience slowly drifted out. A new panel discussion was about to start in the marquee and Rishi decided to get himself a hot cup of coffee. As he walked back from the coffee bar, he found Sir Alistair standing near the fountains, looking somewhat lost.

'Ah, Sir Alistair . . . so pleased to meet you . . . I am one of your biggest fans.'

The poet looked pleased to have discovered an ardent fan in a distant land.

'How I wish I had brought along my copy of *The Deceived & the Garden* for an autograph. What a missed opportunity . . . Are you in India for long?'

'For another week, fly out next Sunday. My first time in the country, so must do my share of sightseeing.'

'Are you free for dinner on Saturday evening by any chance? I would love to host you for a meal. Perhaps we could discuss *Bleany's Garden* over some good wine and authentic home-cooked curry.'

'I get back from Agra on Friday night, so yes, we could do that. Very kind of you.'

Rishi was not quite sure why he had invited Sir Alistair. He had absolutely no interest in late-twentieth-century English poetry. It was just something he had done without thinking. He was wondering what to say next when Ashraf wandered into sight along with the television news presenter who had chaired their session.

'There you are, Alistair. We were looking for you. Care to join us for lunch?'

'I have to go back to my hotel room, but I'll be back here in the evening for the music show . . .'

'Oh no, we both have a flight to catch after lunch . . . what a pity . . .'

Rishi knew of Ashraf—Dolly had dropped his name a few times. The news anchor of course was a well-known face for anyone who flicked channels between 9 p.m. and 11 p.m.

'Well, if I may impose, I have invited Sir Alistair home for dinner on Saturday. I live in Hauz Khas. Would the two of you like to join us?'

And so Rishi ended up hosting a literary gathering in his cousin's house. He also invited Dolly, who was most excited about spending an evening with Ashraf and Sir Alistair.

~

It was the first time that Rishi had invited guests. The cook seemed pleased to be able to show off his skills after a long drought, and was given full rein. A few bottles of decent wine were pilfered from the gallery's stock. Rishi also found a half-full bottle of Laphroaig Single Malt and another of Cockburn's Special Reserve Port in the bar cabinet. He had greater trouble, however, sourcing a copy of *The Deceived & the Garden*. None of the Indian online sites carried Sir Alistair Blackbourne's works. None of the bookshops in Khan Market had a copy. However, Faqir Chand's did manage to dig out another of his works from under the pile at the back of the shop. It had obviously been lying there for some time, as it looked shop-soiled and frayed. Rishi was pleased to acquire it at a discount.

It was one of those cold and misty winter evenings, but the Taneja drawing room was well-lit and warm. The guests arrived, almost all together, at 8 p.m. Drinks and snacks were served. The Bose music system was put to use. The host had been anxious that he would not be able to keep up a literary conversation for a whole evening but he need not have worried. Dolly initially dominated the conversation—she recognized the paintings by Souza, Bawa and Gujral on the walls and pointed them out to the other guests. She dropped names of writers she knew, and flirted gently with Ashraf who seemed to enjoy the wine. The TV anchor loved the snacks and went to the kitchen to ask the cook for more. Sir Alistair nursed his whisky and spoke of his recent sightseeing trips.

By the time dinner was served, everyone was in a jolly mood and the conversation had moved to gossip. Sir Alistair regaled everyone with titbits about the personal lives of famous characters from the sixties and seventies. He was pleased when asked to autograph his book and read out some verses after dinner over a glass of port. The cook had surpassed himself for the main course, but everyone agreed that the home-made kulfi was the crowning moment.

The evening had been a success, and the next day Dolly plastered her Facebook page with photographs. Soon Rishi was part of the social circuit—the cocktail parties, the farmhouse weddings, the private music performances. The former used-car salesman was surprised at how quickly he was absorbed into this new world. He was even more surprised that no one ever asked him about his profession or source of income. It was simply assumed that he had a share in the Taneja business empire. Instead, word got around that he was a great patron of the arts.

It was no more than a few months before Rishi Taneja appeared on his first television debate. He was not sure why he had been asked to provide an opinion on the city's air pollution problem, but social media was unanimous that he was the only one on the panel who had made any sense. Soon, Rishi was being called upon for his opinion on everything from education policy to geo-politics. He soon discovered that he could easily hold his own on most subjects by the simple expedient of looking up Wikipedia before every appearance. He wondered why none of the other participants bothered to do this.

By the time the next winter set in, his Twitter handle had tens of thousands of followers who amplified his opinions. Magazines vied to interview him. His views were particularly sought after in matters of art, culture and lifestyle. A single tweet about a restaurant or fashion boutique could make or break a new establishment. His opinions on literature, similarly, were taken very seriously. Publishers and writers begged him for a blurb. He was flown business class to cities across the country to launch this or that up-and-coming author's new book. Public relations consultants offered him lucrative contracts.

The meteoric rise of Rishi Taneja, however, did not please everyone. Dolly found that she no longer dictated the literary tastes of the national capital and, by extension, the country. She resented the fact that her rambling reviews no longer counted for much against a single line of endorsement, often inane, in a blurb or on social media. It was quite apparent at the cocktail parties that her entourage of hangers-on had switched sides—aspiring poets and writers have a keen sense of such things. However, what she resented most was that he owed it all to her.

So Dolly plotted her revenge. The first step was to find out more about Rishi. She contacted two loyalists who worked as investigative journalists for the *Cavalcade* magazine and asked them to find out more about him. They activated their information networks and, in a few weeks, a picture began to emerge. Certain facts were rechecked by a friend's driver who knew the cook at the Taneja house.

Dolly had expected to find out lurid details about his personal life and business dealings, but what she found was even more damning. Rishi was just a small-town hick from Saharanpur, the son of a shopkeeper who sold paint and pipes. Even worse, he was a failed used-car salesman, not a globe-trotting shareholder in the Taneja business empire, a charity case who had been living off his cousin.

The art gallery and all those expensive paintings on the drawing room wall, none of them belonged to him. What a charlatan!

The next step was to expose and publicly humiliate him. What better place to do this than at the same literary festival where he had started his social ascent. Dolly knew that Rishi had been invited to speak at the event, so she used her old friendships with the organizers to position herself to chair his session. This would allow her to ask him probing questions about his past on a public platform. He would either have to come clean or lie blatantly. Either way, she would ensure that his credibility as a connoisseur of fine dining and fine literature could never be salvaged. She also got the *Cavalcade* to carry a long-form story about him, an exposé of sorts. The magazine would publish its new issue on the same day and it was arranged that copies would be freely distributed at the venue just after their panel discussion.

The day arrived. It was a winter's day with a nip in the air, but sunny. The arrangements were identical to the previous year. Dolly spotted her unsuspecting target enjoying the sun at a table near the coffee bar. She walked up to him and gave him a big hug.

'Hey, you are looking great! I am so looking forward to our session.'

'When you brought me here last year, who would have guessed we would be doing a panel together!'

'Our slot is at 2.30 p.m., please come to the speakers' room a few minutes early to get miked up . . . You know, we'll have fun . . .'

Dolly gave him a big smile before drifting off to the next table where she had spotted an old friend, a theatre director. Rishi continued to sit at the table. A couple of admirers dropped by to speak to him. He had another fifteen minutes to kill and he did not want more coffee. He was wondering if it was worth heading to the marquee to listen to the book reading in progress, when he heard a commotion.

He walked over to the lawns to have a look. There were several police officers on the stage and they were arguing with some of the organizers. One of the panellists, the editor of the *Cavalcade*, was screaming hysterically at the policemen. It was not clear what he was saying, but Rishi caught 'I am innocent' . . . 'all blatant lies' . . . 'I am being targeted' . . . 'she is lying' . . . 'you cannot arrest me' . . . 'I am a feminist' . . . 'this is intolerance' . . . 'Do you not know who I am? I want to speak to the chief minister right now.' This went on for quite some time.

Suddenly, the accused editor jumped off the stage and made a dash for it. It was quite futile, as he tripped and fell on the front row of seats. Two policemen pounced on him and pinned him down before slipping on the handcuffs. They then dragged him away. His shirt was torn from the scuffle. The audience of course watched all this with perverse pleasure and live-streamed it on their phones. A photographer from a local paper asked the policemen to pose with the growling but handcuffed editor; they duly complied.

Matters became clearer only after the police finally left the hotel grounds. It turned out that the editor had been accused of sexually assaulting a colleague the previous night. The young lady had lodged a complaint and the police had decided to take immediate action. Security camera footage at their hotel had captured the whole thing in gory detail. There was no scope for doubt.

The episode completely threw off the event schedule at the literature festival. The organizers were flustered and the audiences distracted. The panel chaired by Dolly was cancelled. It did not take long for television vans and their crew to descend on the venue. As soon as they saw Rishi, a familiar face, they begged him to comment on the dramatic arrest. The former used-car salesman was now in his element. He spent the afternoon describing the sequence of events in dramatic detail to each channel. He did not forget to mention that he had dined a few days earlier with both the accuser and the accused, how he was deeply saddened that such things could happen, and always ended by wisely stating that the law should take its course.

The festival organizers eventually recovered their composure and decided to take advantage of the situation.

A panel on workplace sexual harassment was hurriedly put together. Rishi was a natural choice and he spoke confidently on several aspects of the subject. No one noticed that there were no women on the panel.

Rishi went home pleased that evening. He had thoroughly enjoyed the attention. He would remain blissfully unaware of the boxes of the newly printed issue of the *Cavalcade* that lay forgotten in some corner of the event venue.

Late that night, Rishi sat on the terrace outside his barsati. A full moon covered the rooftops in silver. It was getting cold but he rather liked the bite, a reminder of his days in England. Lazily, he scrolled down the contact list on his phone. It listed the names of the city's rich and famous. His conversion from outsider to insider was complete.

It was just before he went to bed that his cousin Dilip called him from San Francisco.

'Hello, Rishi. Hope you weren't asleep. We haven't spoken in a few months but we see you in the press all the time. You have become quite a celebrity. Well done! I am calling to ask you for a favour. One of my companies is being restructured and needs a new director for the board. I usually don't involve family in my business, but would you consider joining us?'

The Troll

The compound of Sea View Co-operative Housing Society occupied a fifty-yard stretch on a quiet side lane leading off the commercial hustle-bustle of the main road. The name of the housing complex was admittedly a bit misleading as the sea was visible only on low-smog days from the kitchen windows of the top floor in Block B. However, this minor detail would not have deterred its socially ambitious middle-class residents who had recently taken to calling their neighbourhood Greater Juhu rather than Andheri West.

It was almost noon by the time Mrs Deshpande completed the cycle of morning chores. Her daughter had been packed off to college after a heavy breakfast, her husband to office in Bandra-Kurla. The part-time maid had washed the clothes and hung them up in the balcony to dry. She was now free till the family gathered again in the evening.

Mrs Deshpande tied her hair into a bun, picked up her high-power Nikon camera and stepped into the corridor outside her flat. She then took the elevator to the top floor of the building, shutting the collapsible door of the lift as soundlessly as possible, and took a deep breath before examining the landing minutely. Over the next twenty minutes, she walked down the fifteen floors, examining the corridors and stairwell on each floor, taking note of every civic misdemeanour and every maintenance failure: kids' cycles blocking the passage, exposed wires hanging from the ceiling and so on. It was in a corner of the seventh floor that she discovered the outrage: a red streak of tobacco spit splashed below the fire extinguisher. The Nikon was immediately put to use and the evidence photographed from every possible angle, with flash, without flash, long exposure, horizontal frame, vertical frame, zoom in, zoom out. She then continued with the inspection tour. On reaching the ground floor, she glanced suspiciously at the security guards to see if any of them chewed tobacco or paan.

So much evidence of disrepair had been gathered from Block A alone that Block B could wait for another day. Mrs Deshpande downloaded the photographs to her laptop. She then emailed the most incriminating material to Mr Mirchandani, the long-suffering president of Sea View Co-operative Housing Society. While she did not specifically mention Mr Bajaj, the secretary of the maintenance subcommittee, it was obvious from the tone of the mail who was to blame for the unacceptable state of civic decline.

Mr Bajaj and Mrs Deshpande had had a long-running cold war. Matters had escalated a few years earlier after the annual Cultural Day. As secretary of the cultural activities subcommittee, Mrs Deshpande was the main organizer and had put together a full programme of dance, song, drama, poetry reading, all performed by the residents. The programme had included a dance to a somewhat raunchy Bollywood number starring several of the younger female residents, including Mrs Deshpande's daughter, then a pimply teenager. Mrs Deshpande had personally choreographed the moves. The performance had gone well and drawn loud applause, but Mr Bajaj had later remarked that some of the dance moves were perhaps inappropriate for a family event.

Let's say the secretary of the cultural activities subcommittee had taken this personally. Since then she had engaged in a battle of attrition against Mr Bajaj, an otherwise amiable retiree with a shock of grey hair and a thick white moustache. The old man, in turn, had retaliated by blaming every instance of teenage disobedience, from playing loud music at midnight to playing cricket in the car park, on the unwholesome influence of the fifty-year-old housewife.

By the time Mrs Deshpande finished sending the emails to the society president, it was lunchtime. She reheated leftovers from the previous night's dinner and ate quickly. There was no time to waste. After clearing up, she opened her laptop once more. This time she logged into her Twitter and Facebook accounts and was transformed into Bubbly Bento, among the most feared of social media activists. The housewife had discovered this universe quite by chance but now it consumed her. Every day, when her husband and daughter were out, she waged war against all the ills of the world: the deliberately misleading statements of public intellectuals, the blatant lies of well-known journalists, the corruption of politicians and corporate lobbyists, and the hypocrisy of self-proclaimed human rights activists. She pressed home her point with any kind of evidence she could lay her hands on: statistics and references, articles and screenshots of old Facebook or Twitter posts, photographs and long-forgotten YouTube videos. She was relentless. She scoured the Internet for information and gradually built up a trusted support network of anonymous informants who supplied her with facts gleaned from all over the Web. Some of the informants, she did not know quite how, routinely pulled out incriminating documents from old records and private files.

No one knew the true identity of Bubbly Bento but the handle quickly became hugely influential. Even its targets admitted privately that the quality of its research was impeccable. It soon had a legion of ardent followers on all major social media platforms. Supporters and opponents fought pitched battles on its timeline and popular television anchors followed it closely to gauge public mood.

There had been many attempts to guess the identity of Bubbly Bento. Some followers were of the opinion that it was run by a senior diplomat in Delhi while others believed it was a group of bored software professionals in Bengaluru. Then there were those who thought that it was an economist based in Singapore who pretended to be a writer. Mrs Deshpande tracked all this with amusement. She even inserted deliberately misleading updates:

'Edinburgh is so beautiful covered in snow. How I crave a hot cup of tea!'

'When in Manhattan, I always make a pilgrimage to Morimoto.'

'Biryani standards have declined in Lucknow.'

'Electronics have become so expensive in Singapore. Does anyone know a good place to buy a drone?'

The middle-aged housewife sitting in a middle-class Mumbai housing block had never visited any of these cities and had absolutely no intention of buying a drone, but each of these updates set off a flurry of speculation. Meanwhile, her husband and daughter remained blissfully unaware of her online activities. Mr Deshpande worked in an insurance company and held a respectable middle-level position. Ms Deshpande studied commerce and accountancy in a mid-rung college and aspired to follow in her father's footsteps. Both of them would have disapproved of Bubbly Bento. It was one thing to have strong political views in private but quite another to take on the world like this. The only change they had noticed was that the wife/mother appeared to have become unusually well informed about current affairs. Father and daughter were particularly pleased when, at a nephew's wedding, Mrs Deshpande demolished the old family intellectual and shut him up with a barrage of facts and figures. The extended family was deeply grateful but no one thought it necessary to probe further.

The growing social media power of Bubbly Bento, not surprisingly, came to the notice of truenews.in, a blogging site that positioned itself as 'The last refuge of fearless journalism'. In reality, it was run as a sly front for publishing articles that suited the political and commercial interests of those who financed it. Between gossipy articles about Bollywood and scholarly articles on obscure topics, it inserted personal attacks on inconvenient individuals, cleverly couched as investigative journalism. At other times, it lobbied for or against legislation while claiming to espouse high-minded causes like 'social uplift', 'human rights', 'environmental conservation' and 'poverty eradication'. It was of course entirely coincidental that the articles invariably took a stance that helped the cause of one of the website's backers.

When Bubbly Bento began to release details of suspicious accounts held in foreign tax havens, the editors of truenews.in were told to hunt down the person behind it. This was no easy task as Bubbly Bento did not seem to leave any hint of its location. Did it belong to an individual or a group? Were they based in India or abroad? The best in-house hacker failed to crack the password. The references to specific locations were obvious red herrings. It was then that one of the editors noticed that the earliest tweets by Bubbly Bento had included a series of complaints about municipal issues in Mumbai.

Mrs Deshpande had complained bitterly about uncollected garbage and potholes and had attached photographs to prove her point. Those were the days when she was new to social media and inexperienced in its ways. Besides, she had not really been trying to hide her identity at that stage. A careful examination of the photographs suggested that they had been shot on the same road. Indeed, in the background one could clearly discern a signboard announcing 'Sah & Sanghi Auto Agencies, Authorized Dealers'. This was the first clue about the possible location of Bubbly Bento.

The editors of truenews.in handed the investigation over to one of their most promising reporters in Mumbai: Shubhranshu Ghosh Roy, alias Shubho. Around thirty-six years old, he had remained a student at the Film and Television Institute of India for the last fourteen years. Despite the best efforts of his teachers, he had somehow managed not to graduate. Shubho considered himself a misunderstood artist ahead of his time. So, while he waited for times to change, he attached himself to various causes even as he thought of new ways to beg his mother to send him money from Kolkata without informing his ill-tempered father. Unfortunately, the source of funds had become somewhat uncertain after his father began to keep a closer watch on the family finances. This had forced Shubho to take up writing for truenews.in.

Shubho was thin and short. He tried to make up for his stature with oily, unkempt hair that covered his ears and collar but not quite the balding patch near the crown. A few white strands peppered the full beard that ended in a point. Thick-rimmed spectacles completed the picture.

The obvious place to begin the assignment was to scout all the 'Sah & Sanghi' outlets to try and find a match with Bubbly Bento's photographs. A Google maps survey showed Shubho the likely locations and he spent the next few days driving to each of them on a motorcycle borrowed from his roommate. It was on the third day that he discovered the lane. The details matched the photos exactly—the still-overflowing garbage dump, the gulmohar tree and of course the Sah & Sanghi outlet where the lane hit the main road. This was definitely the place. The blogger looked down the lane—there were a couple of grocery shops, a clinic, a dilapidated old bungalow that was probably locked in a legal dispute, a few slum hutments and Sea View Co-operative Housing Society. He came to the conclusion that the housing society was the most likely location of his quarry.

On returning to his hostel room, Shubho reported to the editors that he knew with fair certainty where Bubbly Bento lived, but the editors were not satisfied. They needed the individual to be identified and exposed. The problem was that the housing complex had over ninety apartments and several hundred inhabitants. That evening Shubho poured out his problem to his roomie. The roomie recalled that a former classmate, now a successful advertising executive, had lived in Sea View for several years. This was a stroke of luck!

The very next day Shubho went to meet the advertising executive and pumped him for information about the inmates of Sea View. It was a bit awkward since he could not quite spell out why he needed this information but, in the end, he got what he needed. Mr Bajaj was the obvious suspect—he had once been a compliance officer in a public-sector bank—just the sort who would understand bank accounts and tax havens. A childless widower, he lived alone on the eighth floor in Block B and was known to have conservative views on what women could perform on Cultural Days. Still, Shubho needed personal verification and decided to use an additional piece of information he had gleaned—the fact that Mr Bajaj went for a walk every morning. It would be a good opportunity to observe the man in his natural habitat.

This is how Shubho ended up driving down to Sea View well before dawn. Since he did not know exactly when Mr Bajaj went for his walk, he had no choice but to start his vigil before 6 a.m. Unfortunately, it was the one day in the year when Mumbai enjoyed a nip in the air. Even as he rode the motorcycle through the empty roads, Shubho regretted not bringing along his monkey cap. His mother had long impressed upon him the calamitous effects of catching a chill in the head.

It was still dark when he parked the motorcycle across from Sea View. The gate was left open just enough to let through people but not cars. A security guard was visible through the grilles, slumped over a plastic chair and fast asleep. Everyone in the building seemed to be asleep. Shubho waited, but he was very cold. He again recalled his mother's advice and regretted not bringing the monkey cap. If only he could get a hot cup of tea. He walked tentatively to the end of the lane and looked up and down the main road. Sure enough, there was a man at a small stall stirring milky tea and pumping the stove. What luck! The blogger bought a 'cutting' of tea in a plastic cup and went back to his post. The hot and sugary tea lifted his spirits, but there was still no sign of Mr Bajaj.

About forty minutes into the wait, Shubho faced a new problem. The chill and the tea had conspired to bring his bladder close to bursting. The security guard was still fast asleep, but the sky was brightening and the inhabitants of Sea View were stirring. This was no time to abandon the vigil in search of a toilet; Mr Bajaj could emerge at any moment. There was no real option. Shubho glanced up and down the lane to make sure there was no one around; he looked up and, from what he could see, most of the windows of the blocks were still dark. Then he sidled up to the nearest wall and let loose.

Up on the sixth floor, Mrs Deshpande had just woken up and was preparing tea and breakfast for the family. She peered through the window and saw a bearded man urinating just outside the gate. In a flash, she reached for her trusted Nikon, zoomed in and took a series of high-resolution photographs. She then calmly went back to the toaster.

Having unburdened his bladder, Shubho felt a lot better. A few minutes later, an elderly man with a thick white moustache came out of the gate. He wore a white T-shirt, white tennis shorts, white socks and white sneakers. This matched the description of Mr Bajaj and the blogger followed him at a discreet distance. It was more than a kilometre to the nearest park and the old man kept up a good pace. Shubho was breathless when he arrived. He perched himself on the nearest bench and pretended to fiddle with his smartphone while Mr Bajaj walked vigorously around the park.

By the time the first rays of the sun were filtering through the trees, a motley group of men and women came together in the middle of the park. They all nodded in acknowledgement when Mr Bajaj joined them. He was obviously the ringleader. Then, without any warning, they all burst into laughter. For the next ten minutes, Shubho watched the spectacle of seemingly sensible people going into waves of laughter. He tried to capture the moment as best he could on his smartphone camera. It stopped as suddenly as it had begun and everyone went their own way. The blogger did not bother to keep up with Mr Bajaj back to Sea View; he already had what he needed.

A month later, truenews.in carried a lengthy article exposing Bubbly Bento. It first laid out how social media activists like Bubbly Bento were responsible for the 'post-Truth' world. It detailed how respectable and upright citizens were being harassed by those who dug up their past from the Web. The article then triumphantly announced that it had traced the person behind the abomination: Mr Bajaj—retired public-sector bank employee, former compliance officer, widower and loner. He was known to have expressed conservative views on what teenage girls could perform on Cultural Day. As if all this was not damning enough, the article then presented the clinching evidence of his fascist leanings: Mr Bajaj was the leader of the local laughter yoga club and presided over its morning meetings.

The article was accompanied by a somewhat hazy photograph of a dozen, mostly elderly, men and women laughing in a park, their heads bent back in mirth, their hands holding their bellies. It was signed by Devang Jha, a pseudonym, and included the usual disclaimer: 'The views and opinions expressed in the article are those of the author and do not necessarily reflect those of the staff and editors of truenews.in.'

When the article was posted online, it caused quite a stir. Supporters and opponents of Bubbly Bento passionately debated it and called each other names. For a full day they talked about nothing else, till they moved on to raging about other things. Mr Bajaj, however, remained blissfully unaware of his notoriety. No one with whom he interacted read truenews.in or participated in social media debates—not the members of the laughter club, not the maintenance subcommittee, not the shopkeepers from whom he purchased his grocery.

Of course, Mrs Deshpande did not fail to notice the article. She was most amused by the identification of Mr Bajaj of all people as Bubbly Bento. However, she was also taken aback by how close the investigator had come to finding her. She did not fear what the world would have said if she had been discovered; she was mostly afraid of the scolding that she would have got from both her husband and her daughter for getting mixed up in things that did not concern her. Housing society politics was one thing, national politics was quite another. So she decided to refrain from further social media engagement. She still checked Facebook and Twitter to follow the latest trends but did not type a word. A few weeks later, the editors of truenews.in were able to report to their financial backers that Bubbly Bento had been successfully neutralized.

Mrs Deshpande now focused her energies on preparations for the annual Sea View Society Cultural Day. She supervised the daily practice sessions, balanced the schedule of events to ensure wide participation, negotiated rates with the tent-wala. She deliberately made sure to include a Bollywood dance item performed to 'Sheila ki Jawani' and then roped in Mrs Mirchandani, the president's wife, for the lead role. This was a cunning move calculated to out-manoeuvre Mr Bajaj. The latter knew he had been fixed, but he responded by demanding a slot for a demo of his laughter yoga club. The slot was granted.

The big day arrived. Cars were removed from the parking lot between Blocks A and B, a temporary stage was erected, plastic chairs were laid out, and the mikes and speakers were vociferously checked and rechecked all afternoon. Virtually all the residents gathered at the venue by 7 p.m. The younger children enacted a scene from one of the epics. It was a good performance marred only by the four-year-old dressed as Hanuman who decided, halfway through the battle with Ravan, that he would much rather be with his mother. The teenagers sang popular songs in Hindi and English. As happened every year, the programme took a detour when the audience insisted that Mr and Mrs Bose, the only Bengalis in the neighbourhood, had to sing a song by Tagore. They complied after a ritual show of reluctance and sang the same Rabindrasangeet that they had performed the previous year and the year before. The local poet read out some of his latest compositions. The pieces were competent in Marathi but their literal translations into English were, to put it politely, surreal.

The grand finale was the dance followed by the laughter yoga demo. Thus, the audience was treated to plump middle-aged ladies gyrating to 'Sheila ki Jawani', and then by ten whole minutes of geriatric laughter.

Everyone agreed that this had been the best Cultural Day ever. Even Mr Bajaj congratulated Mrs Deshpande. Over plates of oily pav bhaji, they buried the hatchet. Three months later, Mr Bajaj died peacefully in his sleep. To the end he remained entirely oblivious to his fame in the social media world.

It is not clear how Shubho found out about the death, but a few weeks later he published a condescending obituary in truenews.in. The first half of the piece summarized the previous article but the rest was used, in a somewhat self-congratulatory tone, to hint at how he had played a role in silencing a social media ogre. This time he fearlessly published the article in his own name and even attached a mugshot. Bubbly Bento's supporters and opponents were suddenly reminded of the long-silent handle and spent a few hours debating the propriety of speaking ill of the dead.

Mrs Deshpande too read the article. She then looked at the photograph of the author and felt that she knew the face from somewhere. A quick scan of her old photographs confirmed her suspicions. Here was the same man, in flagrante delicto, exposing his privates in high resolution. She smiled. Then she logged in and, for the first time in months, typed:

'I am still here.'

Of Forbidden Memories

Of who we are
  Of who we're not

Are we the prisoners of our memories?
  But whose memories?
Mine? Or Yours?

Are we the sum total of our stories?
  But whose stories?
Mine? Or Yours?

Of lies that are true
And dreams that are forbidden
Of dreams that are true
And memories that are forbidden

The Bench by the Lake

The lake lies to the south, not far from a once fashionable neighbourhood of a once vigorous city. The city has grown and decayed simultaneously, but the lake still remains. At the end of a hot day, many come here for respite as a cool breeze blows over the water. Toddlers with watchful mothers, lovers half hidden, the occasional band of joggers, fat businessmen walking with their mobile phones pressed to their ears.

The true aristocrats of this world, however, are the elderly men who gather around the park benches nearest to the water's edge. Former schoolteachers, accountants, middle-ranking government officials. Here they come together every evening to dissect the world. The general deterioration in morals, cricket, American foreign policy, delays in road repairs, Brazilian football in the sixties and the exploits of grandchildren.

Over the years, the people have changed but the groups have not. Particular park benches have been passed down through generations of retirees, hierarchy being determined by success in publishing Letters to the Editor in the local newspapers and knowledge of elaborate cures for various conditions. Indignant letters about the state of the roads or the state of the nation. Homoeopathy, naturopathy, allopathy, Tibetan medicine, Unani, Ayurveda . . .

Prabhat Sirkar sat quietly in his usual place on the bench under the old rain tree. He was a tall man, clean-shaven, with a prominent nose and a full head of greying hair. He was in his late seventies; most of his contemporaries had either died or faded away. Two men in their late sixties—both former engineers of the public works department—sat beside him on the bench. Three others stood about them—a retired schoolteacher, an ex-bank teller and a former hotel manager. The former PWD engineers always had strong words about corruption and the general deterioration in morality in public life although the others suspected they too had lined their pockets in their time. The schoolteacher was in the habit of doing impromptu breathing exercises in between his conversations. There were a couple of other 'regulars' who had not come that evening and several others who dropped in occasionally for a chat.

Prabhat had once presided over this assembly but now younger men had usurped his place. No one asked him for his opinions any longer, not even on the arcane workings of an ageing digestive system, a topic on which he considered himself quite an expert. He now retained his place on the bench solely by virtue of seniority of age. He did briefly join an argument about the latest developments in the Israeli–Palestinian conflict but the discussion turned to a more mundane one about the proposal to increase electricity tariffs. Someone offered to write a strongly worded letter to the editor of the *Statesman*. No one noticed when Prabhat got up to leave. In the fading light, he walked down the path leading back to his apartment. Other than a persistent stiffness in his left knee, he was in good shape for his age. It was not his body but his mind that felt weighed down. He had walked down this path for years but today he knew he was seeing all this for the last time.

The path turned into a footpath past the White Border Cricket Club. Boys and girls in white were doing stretching exercises. Prabhat could hear the coach enthusiastically coaxing along his team. He then crossed a busy intersection. After walking a quarter of a mile along a busy, noisy road at rush hour, he turned left into a narrow lane just before the new Toyota showroom. He passed the hawker selling cigarettes and paan. Another fifty yards, and he stopped in front of a three-storey house with a fading sign that still proclaimed his father: Jagadish Prasad Sirkar, Advocate, High Court.

The house had been built seventy years ago by the successful lawyer. He had wanted Prabhat to follow in his footsteps but the son had shown little interest in law. He wanted to be a poet, a revolutionary writer who transcended these petty bourgeois pursuits, but economic necessity meant that he had to live at home and bear his father's disappointments. Marriage and then a daughter, the death of the parents, all that was many decades ago. Only the daughter was alive now, married to a Gujarati businessman in Mumbai. He had not heard from them in years. Prabhat had objected to the match—he no longer cared why but it had caused a wound that never healed.

Prabhat fumbled for his keys, found them and unlocked a door that opened on to a staircase. It was dark but he could hear his former tenants—talking, watching television, scrubbing pots and pans in the kitchen. He now lived in a single large room with a wide balcony. It had been his father's study. Even now it had large teak bookcases along the walls although the books on law had long been sold off. The rest of the house was now inhabited by strangers who had first paid rent but then gradually bought off the place bit by bit.

It was quite dark now, but the old man did not switch on the light. Instead he walked instinctively to the balcony and sat down on the armchair. There he gathered his memories. The years of trying to publish, the occasional successes, the brief period of fame when he became a poet of the revolution, the party work, the student insurrection and its brutal suppression, then finally the long fading away. Many of the revolutionary leaders had been arrested, some even killed. They had come for him as well but his father had used his influence to shield him. Prabhat and his young family had to live four years in exile with relatives in London. He spent this time working on some short-term research projects for the School of Oriental and African Studies. There were a few other exiles like him and they met regularly in an Arab-run cafe to discuss their return. In reality, few went back. One former revolutionary went on to create a successful retail chain in America, a glorified shopkeeper. Prabhat disdained commerce and found it difficult to come up with a suitable source of income. The hospitality of his hosts gradually wore thin. Eventually, he and his family returned home.

Things had calmed down by then. Most of the remaining party faithful had drifted away. The few who were still active in politics had joined mainstream parties and would go on to hold high office. Only a handful stayed committed to the revolution but they too shunned Prabhat. They accused him of having deserted them.

Nobody remembered all this now, or cared. Someone had told him that his songs were still sung by those who kept alive the revolutionary spirit in remote forest hamlets although they probably did not know who had composed them. All these memories—so far, and yet so vivid and close. But tomorrow would be a new day.

Prabhat woke up as usual at eight thirty. The boy brought his morning tea. The lawyers arrived at ten with the final documents and the money in cash. His former tenant had bought the rest of the house in bits and pieces, now he could have it all. The teak shelves, the bed, the gas stove and the old armchair had also been purchased by him.

Prabhat had already packed his remaining belongings into an old-fashioned metal trunk. The trunk was a battered black but had acquired bright red handles after repairs a few years earlier. The old man divided the money carefully between the trunk and a smaller suitcase that also contained his precious supply of homoeopathic pills. The boy helped place the heavy trunk in the boot of the yellow Ambassador taxi.

The trunk was large and awkward, and did not fit neatly into the boot. However, the driver was used to excess baggage. Without a word, he produced a rope that secured the top to the bumper. The suitcase was placed on the front seat. Prabhat tipped the boy well and then they drove off to the railway station. The old Ambassador rattled as it lurched through the midday traffic. It was steaming hot as the taxi was not air conditioned but that did not bother the old man. His mind was far away. It took over an hour to cross the bridge and reach the station. He paid the fare, stared distractedly as the embarrassed taxi driver helped him with a jammed door handle, and then hailed a porter to carry his luggage.

~

Saligram is a small university town. The train journey took four hours. As the train neared the town, the paddy fields gave way to wooded hills covered with the tall sal trees that gave the town its name. The university had seen better days but the town of Saligram had grown somewhat bigger and more crowded than he remembered it. The old arches of the colonial-era railway station remained the same.

'Are you Mr Rathin Dasgupta by any chance?'

'Ah, Arnab, it was very kind of you to come to receive me at the station.'

'Arrey, not at all.'

'As you can see, I have this large trunk. It has everything I own now. Hope it will fit in your car. I had trouble fitting it into the boot of the taxi.'

'No problem. It's amazing what one can shove through the hatch of a Maruti Alto once you lower the rear seats.'

He was right; the porter had little difficulty pushing the black steel trunk with red handles into the rear of the hatchback.

Arnab Talukdar's home was on the outskirts of Saligram. It was a whitewashed, single-storey house with a small garden in front. Potted plants of every size bordered the lawn, giving the impression of enthusiasm rather than talent. There was a vegetable patch at the back and beyond it was a small, freestanding building with a room and an attached bathroom. This is where Arnab led his new tenant.

'Hope you do not find this place disappointing. As agreed, we will provide the meals. The maid can bring them to you or you can eat with us.'

'The room looks fine. I will pay at the beginning of every month, in cash. Do you get any newspapers that I can borrow after you have read them?'

'Of course. Remember, I am a journalist. I get the local paper in the morning and the city dailies arrive by train before lunch. You are very welcome to read them.'

Rathin settled quickly into his new life. He read the local newspaper in the morning, the city dailies after lunch and went for leisurely walks before dusk. Often he ate dinner with the Talukdar family—the journalist, his schoolteacher wife and their seven-year-old son. Then the adults watched television together and chatted till it was time to retire at ten. In no time, Rathin became a part of his landlord's family. He sometimes helped the seven-year-old with his homework or even took him to watch an animation film or two at the new mall. He offered gardening tips to the boy's mother. In the casual hypochondria of Bengalis, they discussed symptoms of various ailments and Rathin would offer homoeopathic remedies in small glass vials.

~

The summer heat was followed by the relief of the rains and then the months cooled. The journalist occasionally took the train to the city to meet his editor or watch a live performance that he had to review. Some days he worked from the local office, on others he worked on a laptop from home. It was during these occasions that he discovered that his tenant was quite a store of literary knowledge. Arnab enjoyed discussing his book reviews and articles with him. In fact, he often told the older man that he should have been a writer or a poet.

One day in late January, Rathin broke his routine to go down to the city for the day—he left early in the morning and returned late at night. He did not tell anyone where he had been and the Talukdars were too polite to ask. A few days later, the following obituary appeared in all the main newspapers:

In Loving Memory of Prabhat Sirkar, 1939–2015
Poet & Visionary
May He Rest In Peace
He will be missed by Family, Friends and all those who were Inspired by his Works.

(Below was a black-and-white photograph of the deceased from his mid thirties: an unruly beard and somewhat dishevelled hair as became a true revolutionary.)

When Rathin returned from his daily walk, he saw Arnab sitting on the lawn with a laptop and a cup of tea. The city dailies lay in a pile near his feet.

'Working from home this afternoon?'

'Yes. The sun was bright—much better working on the lawn than in a cold, gloomy office.'

'Have you seen the papers today—about Prabhat Sirkar? Perhaps you youngsters no longer remember him, but he was a great influence in the late sixties—a great revolutionary poet—he died yesterday. Quite a loss.'

Rathin picked up one of the papers and pointed out the obituary.

'The name sounds vaguely familiar but I can't claim to have read his works.'

'I knew him well from childhood. Very remarkable man. I still have a collection of his works in my trunk.'

'May I borrow it? Sounds like a great idea for an article—I have been looking for ideas. Perhaps you can fill in the details of his life.'

'Of course. As I said, I knew him well . . . even have a photograph somewhere.'

So it came to be that the article appeared in the city's leading newspaper. It gave a glowing account of Prabhat Sirkar's life, the passion of his words, his influence on his times. Many people read it. Suddenly, emeritus professors in the university remembered their student days and septuagenarian politicians recalled the protest pickets of their youth. These were followed by other articles, and still others. Even those who had never heard of Prabhat Sirkar claimed to have known him well and to have been deeply moved by his poetry. A publisher promised to print a complete collection of his works.

At a press conference, the minister of culture and education said he would commission a bust of the poet for a city park. It was proposed to be placed in the middle of what was used as a football field by the neighbourhood boys and attracted furious protests from the local community. The literature department at the university promised to include the 'great revolutionary poet' in its new, revised syllabus. Friends and relatives emerged from nooks and crannies; Letters to the Editor were sent in from the bench by the lake. A well-known artist even announced an exhibition of paintings inspired by the poetry of the recently deceased.

~

As abruptly as it had begun, the clamour died down. The poet's bust was never ordered and local football matches continued uninterrupted in the park. The university literature syllabus remained unchanged, the artist painted a glamorous actress and the publisher eventually opted for a series of romantic novels that were certain to be popular with teenage girls.

. . . But it did not matter to Prabhat Sirkar. He had followed it all from Saligram and was satisfied. He knew that he was now immortal at his bench by the edge of the lake. For years to come, he would be discussed under the old rain tree: many an anecdote would be told about him, many an aphorism and miraculous remedy ascribed to him.

Life over Two Beers

It was Friday evening. The bars and restaurants at Boat Quay were quickly filling up as lawyers, bankers, accountants, traders, market analysts and consultants poured out of the surrounding offices. It had been a rough week, a rough month and a rough year for anyone connected to financial markets. All over the world, equity indices had fallen sharply and bonds threatened to default. Boat Quay had seen its heyday in the nineties. The tourists and the hip crowd had moved to Clarke Quay, Marina Bay and other places. Despite the relative decline and the recession, however, Boat Quay still attracted a steady clientele from the financial district and, on a Friday night, it was almost as lively as in the old days.

Amit sat alone at a table near the water's edge. From here he could watch the milling crowds without being fully visible in the semi-darkness. Many of those walking past were colleagues or people he had known during his decade in Singapore, but Amit was in no mood to talk to anyone. Snatches of conversation wafted in from nearby tables.

'I think the Dow will fall another 2 per cent tonight . . . just look at the futures . . .'

'Bank of America is a good buy at this level . . . Yes, get us two pitchers of Tiger.'

'It has been two weeks since the con-call and we still don't have the bloody contract.'

'Yeah, yeah, you told us to buy it when it was twelve and now it's six . . .'

'Pick me up at seven tomorrow and let's see if we can play all eighteen holes . . .'

'I don't care if the GDP is still growing 7 per cent, I don't believe those Chinese numbers.'

The scene was familiar, the conversations were familiar, the people were familiar but it felt unreal and dreamlike. It was as if it was all an illusion—the laughter, the office talk, the pretensions, the gentle ribbing of old buddies, the designer handbag hung nonchalantly on the chair. Amit ordered another beer and wondered whether or not to get something to eat. He did not feel hungry.

He had been in conference calls all day with the big boys of the London office. It was all over. There had been rumours for several weeks and hectic last-ditch efforts to save the firm. The rescue package, however, fell apart as investors deemed the liabilities too open-ended and the assets of uncertain value. The share price had plunged to a fraction of its peak. Earlier in the day, amidst the growing financial turmoil, the regulators had decided Amit's firm was not large enough to be of systemic importance and could be allowed to fail. He wondered how many of his colleagues and friends drinking in the nearby bars and pubs already knew this. It did not matter for it would be all over the papers and newswires by Monday morning.

Amit Menon was in his late thirties, slim and fit—the sort that ran a marathon every year and pretended to enjoy it. Although his parents came from a small town in Kerala, he had grown up in middle-class Mumbai. Soon after finishing his MBA from Ahmedabad, he had joined the financial industry and had spent over a decade trading bonds in Singapore. He was no star trader but had proved competent and conscientious enough to be entrusted with a modest trading book of his own. There had been one or two relationships but they had not gone anywhere and Amit remained unmarried. He had been paid enough to rent a comfortable two-bedroom apartment off River Valley Road and to indulge in a couple of expensive holidays every year somewhere in the world. Although he had come nowhere close to earning the million-dollar bonuses that had been whispered about during the boom years, he had had little reason to complain. On the whole, life seemed to have treated him quite well until now.

However, sipping his beer that Friday evening, Amit felt resentful and let down—by those commodity traders in New York and London who had gambled the firm's entire capital base on a one-way bet. What were they thinking? And by the senior managers who should have known what was going on. Besides, what were the guys in risk management doing? They always asked him so many questions for the most innocuous of trades but had not bothered to look at the hundreds of millions, perhaps billions, of dollars being lost by the senior traders. He was sure that investigations would reveal more than bad judgement—possibly illegal transactions, collusion and hidden accounts.

He ordered another beer and a plate of satay. Thoughts drifted back to when he had first come to Singapore— the group of young professionals with whom he used to hang out. Some locals and some expatriates, they worked in the financial district, all on their first job, and drank excessively over the weekend. The live band at EscoBar had been a favourite. It had shut down years ago but Amit remembered the many evenings he had spent there in the early years. Then there was the cheap Roti-Prata place in one of the back alleys. He had not been there in years and wondered if it had been replaced, as often happened, by an upscale restaurant.

The weekend passed peacefully enough. Amit spent it going for long runs in Bukit Timah Nature Reserve just to purge himself of that sinking feeling through sheer physical exhaustion. As expected, the headlines on Monday morning broke the news to the world. His mobile phone kept ringing as friends, acquaintances and rivals called to ask what had happened. Amit answered only a couple of his closest friends . . . he knew that most were calling for gossip rather than any genuine concern for his well-being.

There were weepy scenes when he dropped into the office. Although rumours of the firm's demise had been circulating for some days, it was still a shock to many employees. The top management had been called in by the Monetary Authority of Singapore, but the others sat around the office. Some still hoped for a last-minute rescue package but by lunchtime a notice was pasted on the glass door of the trading room, which made it clear that it was all over. It also listed a handful of employees who would be retained for the liquidation process. Amit was not one of them. So that was it. He cleared his desk and put his personal items into a cardboard box. He then walked over to Sue Lin in HR and handed in his company laptop and BlackBerry.

'Presume I won't get that million-dollar bonus this year.'

'No time for humour, Amit . . . this is just terrible, terrible . . . just cannot believe it.'

'You know where to contact me if you need me . . . my Gmail is the best place.'

'Let's say goodbye properly. Some of us are meeting at five at the Kopitiam . . . Coffee and kaya toast to drown our sorrows. Come, join us . . .'

'Can, *lah*. See you there.'

Amit knew he was without a job and had only modest savings—most of his wealth had been locked up in company stocks that were now worthless. Finding another job in a collapsing financial industry was out of the question. Given the recent experience, he was not sure if he wanted to stay in the industry anyway. He was grateful that at least he was not burdened with a mortgage or a dependent family. He wondered what he would do next. Would he start all over again? He needed to get away and clear his head. He needed to 'find' himself.

After he had finished packing and clearing his apartment, Amit was surprised by how little he would have to carry with him. He even got a fair price for the car, an expensive indulgence in Singapore. The furniture, kitchen gadgets and the home-theatre system belonged to the landlord. He gave away the few bottles of wine and spirits to friends along with plates, glasses and cutlery. The books and music DVDs fit into two cardboard boxes which he shipped to his parents' home in Mumbai. All that remained were clothes, toiletries, shoes and so on. They fit easily into two large suitcases and a rucksack, barely more than what he had brought with him over a decade earlier. He loaded them into the taxi. As the taxi made its way to Changi Airport, Amit felt a big load lift from his shoulders. He suddenly felt free.

The flight to Delhi was uneventful. The city was baking in the extreme heat of June but the former bond trader had no intention of staying there for long. He bought a sackful of books from Bahri's and Faqir Chand's in Khan Market and booked himself on a flight heading further north to Ladakh.

Although it is the main market town in Ladakh, Leh is a tiny place nestled in a small valley between some of the world's highest mountains. Sunlight looks and feels different at this altitude. The stark mountains, bereft of all vegetation, were still capped with snow in June. Amit knew he had to spend two days in Leh to acclimatize. He leisurely explored the main bazaar, buying supplies, sipping mint tea at the German Bakery and walking up to the recently repaired old palace. Although there had been a sharp increase in the number of tourists visiting Leh in recent years, the town still had the feel of an outpost at the edge of the world.

Amit wanted to head out further. On the third day, he hired a jeep to take him to Khardung La—at a height of almost 5400 m—and then onward to the remote Nubra Valley. As the vehicle descended into the valley, he was rewarded with a sight that no tourist brochure could do justice to. The Shyok River, swollen by the melting glaciers, rushed between the dry, desolate, rocky slopes of the mountains. Here and there were scattered hamlets surrounded by fields of a shade of bright green that he would have thought impossible had he not seen it for himself.

Amit had rented a small room in one of the village homes for six weeks. It was sparsely furnished but clean, and the landlady provided breakfast and dinner. The door opened on to a small orchard and a winding path then led down to the river. One could sit on a grassy mound and toss pebbles into the gushing water. This was just what Amit needed. Most days, after breakfast, he packed his rucksack with a bottle of water, some food and a couple of books and then went for long walks into the surrounding hills. Over the next few weeks he explored Buddhist monasteries, nearby hamlets and valleys, and even made friends with soldiers manning a lonely military post. Cut off from news from the rest of the world, Amit felt himself return to balance.

About two weeks into this, the former bond trader found himself at a beautiful spot just outside the village. A narrow stream flowed under a wooden footbridge. On one side were green fields and on the other was a small apricot orchard. Amit pulled out two bottles of beer that he had brought with him and put them to chill in the freezing glacial melt of the stream, taking care to secure them with stones so that they did not get washed away. Then, with his feet in the sun and his head in the shade of a tree, he settled into Peter Hopkirk's *Trespassers on the Roof of the World: The Secret Exploration of Tibet*.

Perhaps an hour had gone by when Amit looked up to see a young woman standing a few feet away. She was obviously not a local. Tall and slim, she wore her hair short like that of a schoolboy; her eyes were lined with kohl. Although not conventionally beautiful, there was something about her that was refreshing and attractive. He smiled and she returned the smile.

'Hi! Here on holiday?'

'You can say that . . . a long holiday . . . Been here for two weeks and intend to hang around for four weeks more.'

'It is a beautiful place to just hang around. And I see that you have arranged for your own supply of beer.'

'Yes . . . I have two bottles and I'm happy to share.'

The beer was chilled and refreshing. Amit learned that the woman's name was Aditi—'Everyone calls me Addy'—and that she worked for an NGO that supported a village school in Nubra Valley. She had come up from Delhi for a few weeks to write a report on how the project was progressing and was staying in the next hamlet. They sat there chatting long after the beer was finished, till the afternoon sun was replaced by the biting chill and bright stars of a Ladakhi evening.

Amit and Addy met almost every day. Addy spent the mornings in the school but in the afternoons they went walking together along the valley. On Sundays they hired a jeep to visit Leh. After Nubra, Leh felt like a big, noisy city. They ate the fresh bakes and drank mint tea at the German Bakery, purchased supplies and even picked up newspapers, usually a day old, to find out how the world was getting along. Amit listened with fascination to Addy as she spoke of her work at the NGO, her artist friends and the bohemian life of Delhi's 'party' set. She had grown up mostly in Delhi and seemed to know everyone who mattered. Her father had been a senior civil servant, and her mother a well-known professor of sociology who had served as a member of various government committees. There was a brother, a journalist, who now lived somewhere in the United States. Addy did not seem to like her brother but did not explain why.

~

The peaches and apricots were sweet in August but they were also a reminder that the weather would soon turn and Ladakh would slide into one of the most extreme winters experienced on this planet. Only the hardy locals and the soldiers would remain to face it. Addy prepared to return home to Delhi, and Amit, still unsure of what he wanted to do, followed her there.

To pay the bills, he took up a consultancy project offered by an old friend from business school. It was light work and it left him with plenty of time to explore a city he barely knew. He also rented a tiny apartment in Saket, close to a metro station. He met Addy often—at Khan Market for coffee, shopping or a movie in Saket, drinks at Hauz Khas Village, art exhibitions at Triveni Kala Sangam and long walks in Lodhi Gardens.

As the weather cooled into October, Delhi's social life suddenly came alive. Wine tastings at the European embassies, music festivals amidst medieval ruins, book launches at India Habitat Centre, farmhouse parties on the outskirts of the city. Plenty of free food and drink for those lucky enough to be invited. Addy led Amit into this world. Suddenly he was in the same room as writers, politicians, journalists, diplomats and businessmen he had only ever read about or seen on television.

'Ah, Addy, so nice to see you. That's a lovely *jamavar* you're wearing . . . looks familiar, your mother has a similar one.'

'Yes, I borrowed it from Mom for the evening.'

'How's Dad? I was supposed to play a round of golf with him last weekend, but you know how it is . . . Had to go to Jodhpur for the Sufi music festival.'

'Dad is fine. He was supposed to be here, but had to go for cocktails at the Italian embassy. He'll probably drop by later.'

'And won't you introduce me to the young man here?'

'Yes, of course! This is my friend Amit. He has just moved to Delhi from Singapore.'

'Ah, Singapore—far too clinical for my taste. Are you originally from Delhi?'

'No, sir, I grew up in Mumbai.'

'Bombay! I am off to Bombay next week for Christmas. My sister lives there . . . Vimala Ramani. Do you know her? Everyone in Bombay seems to know her.'

'No, sir, I don't know her.'

'She has a lovely apartment in Malabar Hill . . . fine views of the Arabian Sea . . . and the most excellent collection of Tanjore paintings. You should drop in and see them. And meet my nephew . . . a bit younger than the two of you. Just finished from Princeton. Very talented boy . . . wants to be a writer like his uncle. And where did you study?'

'IIT, electrical engineering . . . then IIM Ahmedabad.'

'Ah, engineering, finance. Did you also go to Cathedral? My nephew was at Cathedral.'

'No, sir, I attended Kendriya Vidyalaya in Mankhurd.'

'Mankhurd? Where is that?'

'Not far from Chembur, I grew up in Chembur.'

'Is that near the airport? . . . Ah, I see Bunny, I need to speak to her about a Ford Foundation project. Addy, if you will excuse me.'

Although he got no more than occasional snatches of conversation with these luminaries, Amit was star-struck by the easy access to celebrities. He was also surprised by the clubby fraternity between people who tore into each other in newspaper op-eds and television debates.

Addy's circle of friends lived their lives on the periphery of this world of the rich, the powerful and the famous. There was Palash—thin, spectacled, with a wispy beard and long, curly hair—who had dropped out of architecture school nine years earlier because he wanted to write a novel. The book was almost done and Palash claimed to be negotiating with a large publishing house. Meanwhile, he was supporting himself by writing freelance on fashion, food and whatever took his fancy, and by the simple expedient of continuing to live with his parents in Safdarjung Enclave.

Addy's best friend was Mala. In her mid thirties, she was short and somewhat overweight and worked for a foreign-funded development agency that engaged with village communities. Her hair was always closely cropped, a large red bindi in the middle of her forehead, thick kohl lining her eyes, chunky faux-tribal earrings. Amit met her for the first time at a dinner party on the terrace of her barsati. He complimented her on a handwoven, ethnic stole that she was wearing and was told that it was 'fresh off the loom' from one of the villages where she worked.

Zara was doing a PhD in peace and gender studies from some university in the US—or was it the UK?—and had been in India for the last five years for her fieldwork. Meanwhile, she also held a research position at a think tank and did projects for Addy's NGO. Her father had been a well-known journalist in the nineties.

Then there was Tim, the India correspondent of a British newspaper, who liked to talk incessantly about his love for Urdu poetry. He was a bit older than the rest, mid forties, and often wore Indian clothes in the self-conscious Merchant–Ivory sort of way. Amit discovered that the others gave Tim a lot of respect as he was the source of all the invitations to the embassy wine tastings.

There were several others who came and went—a couple of painters, an experimental film-maker, a lecturer and a TV journalist who told the funniest of stories from his coverage of election campaigns across India. Amit enjoyed this new world, far removed from that of his previous life. Delhi's social life was fabulous in winter—and it was fabulous to be a part of it even if he could feel his girth expanding from all the alcohol and rich food. In his free time, he explored Delhi's many ruins, reminders that even the greatest empires are mortal. He wondered about his relationship with Addy and where it was headed.

~

As March turned to April, the days became abruptly warmer. Early one morning, Addy called Amit to ask him to come to her office. Her NGO, People's Action Network, wanted to apply for new grants from a US-based foundation and needed someone to write out a proposal. They were in a hurry to meet the deadline and all the staffers were already tied up. She wondered if Amit, with his MBA, could do the job. Although the organization did not pay market rates, he would be given something for it.

A few hours later, Amit reported to the office in India Habitat Centre. He had to meet Addy's boss, Mrs Rudra, a formidable lady in her late fifties, who had founded the organization. No conference in Delhi was complete without her, and Amit saw her quoted in the papers all the time. If anything, he felt a bit intimidated by this lady with streaky grey hair tied in a tight bun and a large red bindi on her forehead. However, the project seemed straightforward enough. It required him to make the case for a US$2-million grant for AIDS prevention in Nadia district. He would be provided with data to support the case but he would have to write the text, make projections, estimate costs and prepare charts.

After that, Amit spent a part of the day in Addy's office. As temperatures rose steadily, the city's social life shifted to small, private gatherings in air-conditioned drawing rooms. The well-heeled began packing for their summer breaks in Europe or up in their Himalayan retreats. For those who relied on invitations to sponsored events, this was the lean season.

Addy's set was one of those affected by the social slowdown but Amit was surprised to find that he was relieved. He had begun to tire of the same conversations, the posturing and the finely coded language used by insiders to put down those they considered socially inferior. Then there was the slavish imitation of the 'arty look'—the absurd uniformity of those who wished to be different in exactly the same way. He had even come to know the exact price of the Fabindia apparel passed off as 'fresh off the loom'. He was especially grateful that Tim and Zara, now lovers, had temporarily discontinued their fortnightly readings of nineteenth-century Urdu love poetry.

The artists, academics and social workers who had seemed so refreshingly different now appeared bitchy and banal. In fact, he realized that they spoke obsessively about money all the time—of grants that they had landed or should have landed and of sponsorships from companies and governments that they loudly denounced in public. The journalist's election-campaign stories no longer seemed amusing after he had heard the same punchline from half a dozen other scribes. Even Addy, who had looked so cool and refreshing in Ladakh, seemed increasingly commonplace and perhaps even mildly irritating in Delhi. Many of her ideas, often passionately and loudly argued, now seemed a thoughtless repetition of opinions held by her group.

Thus, there was little to distract the former bond trader as he dug into his new project. He was provided data on field surveys of HIV infection in Nadia district where Mrs Rudra wanted to start the new project. Using results from Oral Rapid Tests on several hundred people in the area, the NGO's researchers had argued that HIV was dangerously widespread. A few days later he was also provided before-and-after data on Vaishali district where the NGO had earlier done a very successful project. Amit was expected to use the results of the new survey to make a case for large-scale intervention in Nadia and then leverage the success of the old project to pitch for the grant.

Amit began to systematically make his way through the information. Since he was new to the field, he also spent time trying to understand the various tests used to detect HIV and all the strategies used to tackle the problem. After several days of trawling through the field data and googling information on the subject, Amit found that the pieces somehow did not quite fit together. When he asked more questions of others in the office, they initially answered politely but after a while the general tone suggested that he was unnecessarily delving into too many details and should get on with finishing the proposal as soon as possible. Still, there was something that bothered him.

The HIV surveys for the new project in Nadia had been done using Oral Rapid Tests. This is a quick and cheap test that is supposed to be 99 per cent accurate. This sounds very accurate to those unused to dealing with statistics. Consider the following illustration. Say, the survey is done in an area where there is one person in a thousand who is infected. When the test is carried out on a representative sample of 10,000 people, it would very likely identify the ten-odd infected persons. Since the test is only 99 per cent accurate, however, it will also falsely identify another 100 uninfected people as infected (what is called a 'false-positive'). In other words, the survey results would magnify the HIV infection rate by an order of magnitude even if the tests were carried out correctly and there were no major sampling errors. The reality was almost certainly worse since field conditions in rural India likely caused error rates that were much higher than ideal laboratory conditions. When such a survey was used to make projections for a district like Nadia with a population of 5–6 million, one ended up with tens of thousands of people who were false-positives.

From what Amit understood, the right thing to do would be to reconfirm the results using other tests such as ELISA in order to eliminate the false-positives from the data. When he made discreet inquiries about whether or not confirmation tests had been done, he discovered that the organization had not bothered to conduct them on the grounds that these would require a lot more time and money. This meant that the infection rates were being exaggerated and the grant application was based on a gross misrepresentation of facts.

Having discovered this discrepancy, Amit decided to look more closely at the data for the earlier project in Vaishali. He found that the same Oral Rapid Tests had been used to estimate infection rates at the beginning of the project. Not surprisingly, it showed up tens of thousands of infected people. Three years later, the same survey was repeated but this time, those identified by the oral test were made to undergo an additional confirmation test. This weeded out most of the false-positives. As a result, the reported infection rate dropped dramatically. The NGO then claimed that its campaign had saved thousands of lives.

At first, Amit could not believe what he had found and wondered if he should take Addy into confidence. However, he decided to dig a bit deeper to confirm his suspicions. He requested for the registers with the names of those tested in Vaishali. The person in charge of office records initially said he had forgotten where such old information was stored—in fact, he thought that the registers were probably lost. Amit, however, insisted that they were critical for making the new grant application. Eventually, after much cajoling, he was taken to a dusty and dark storeroom and told that the relevant registers lay somewhere in the piles of paper and documents.

After an hour of searching among the dusty files, Amit finally found a stack that contained all the Vaishali-related paperwork. He took them to his desk and began to scan the names systematically. It was tough going—the names were handwritten by different people, often in a hurry. Sometimes the entry was in English and sometimes in Hindi. Furthermore, many people shared the same name and one had to spend time cross-checking addresses or, where recorded, their father's names. It was almost midnight by the time he was able to collate enough data to make his case. He had found many entries shown as HIV-infected in the first survey but declared uninfected in the survey done three years later. These cases were obviously false-positives. For all the progress made in slowing the spread of HIV and using medication to control its symptoms, the virus was still incurable. Thus, these people had clearly never been HIV carriers in the first place.

With his suspicions confirmed, Amit wanted to keep working on the data. There was no one around in the office at that late hour, so he slipped the registers into his bag and took them home for the weekend. After breakfast on Saturday morning, he sat at his dining table and opened all the books. Within a couple of hours he found several dozen more cases of false-positives who had been miraculously cured by the NGO. A simple statistical analysis showed that all the improvement claimed by the NGO in Vaishali could be explained entirely by the fact that the post-project survey had done an additional confirmation test. In other words, the NGO did not merely overstate the AIDS situation in

Vaishali and Nadia, it was also lying about the effectiveness of its project in Vaishali.

All alone in his flat, Amit wondered what he should do next. He could take the matter directly to Mrs Rudra. Surely she would immediately recognize the problem. Alternatively, he could ask Addy for advice. As he sat there trying to make up his mind, he noticed a piece of paper sticking out of the file. It turned out to be a letter addressed to Mrs Rudra, sent about two years earlier, from someone called Krishna Kumar.

Amit picked up the letter and sat back on his bed to read it, but he turned cold when he realized that the writer had explained the problem with the Vaishali project in some detail. So Mrs Rudra was definitely aware of the issue.

Now, who was this Krishna Kumar? The letter seemed to suggest someone who worked in the NGO but so far he had not met anyone by that name in the office. Wondering how to identify this person, Amit typed the name into Facebook search. Several Krishna Kumars popped up but one of them had two friends in common. His old photos confirmed that he had once worked at India Habitat Centre. This must be the man. It required no more than a phone call to one of the common friends to get hold of his mobile number.

'Hello, is that Krishna Kumar?'

'Yes, speaking.'

'My name is Amit Menon and I am a consultant at People's Action Network. I am helping them with an AIDS-related proposal and came across a letter you had written about their Vaishali project. I need to speak to you about it.'

'What do you want to know? . . . I left them two years ago . . . I am not sure I want to talk about it.'

'Please, please help me. I have found evidence that supports your argument.'

'So what? I no longer have anything to do with them.'

'Look, I just need to speak to you . . . in private . . . just the two of us. Let me buy you dinner.'

'. . . Mmm . . . Okay. Where?'

'How about Rajinder da Dhaba, say at eight?'

'I will be there . . .'

Amit arrived a few minutes before 8 p.m. It was already crowded but he managed to find a spot outside, on one of the permanently parked scooters that are used as informal seating. He recognized his guest as soon as he took off his motorcycle helmet. Krishna Kumar was wearing a loose T-shirt and jeans—the sort that are sold cheap in heaps in Sarojini Nagar Market and are ubiquitously worn by Delhi's college students.

'Hi, thanks for coming.'

'No problem. I now work nearby in Bhikaji Cama for a small trading company.'

'Quite a change from working at People's Action Network!'

'Well, not quite . . . I am in admin, not an activist. I used to be in PAN's admin department as well.'

'So how did you get involved in the Vaishali project?'

'I am from Vaishali . . . to be more precise, my parents came to Delhi from there. I was born here in Delhi. Grew up in Moti Bagh.'

'So you must know Addy and Mala from childhood. I believe they grew up there too.'

'Ha ha . . . not quite. They are children of senior officers. I grew up in the servants' quarters. My father was a driver and my mother was a cook. I earned a BCom from one of the lesser-known colleges . . . must admit, I barely passed. I took the first job I got . . . that was at PAN.'

'Let's place the order first. Here is the menu. What would you like?'

'Kadai murg? Maybe some dal tadka?'

'Great. Let's add some butter naan. We can order more if we are still hungry.'

'Now to return to the Vaishali project. As I said, I was a junior accountant in office admin and was not directly involved with it in any way. However, by chance the survey was done in my village and my aunt happened to be one of those who were tested. She tested positive. Nothing remains hidden in a village and, as you know, there is a lot of stigma attached to being HIV-positive. Her life became hell . . .'

'I can imagine!'

'She is a semi-literate village woman. Very loving. But had no idea about the whole AIDS thing. It was as if lightning had struck the family. Luckily her husband was supportive and called me to find a doctor in Delhi to cure her. As I heard them out, I realized that the tests had been done by my own employer. So, I went and asked one of the field workers who told me not to worry and simply get a confirmatory test done. My aunt went to a private clinic in the nearby town and got the additional test done. It was expensive but she was all clear. A false-positive.'

'My god! That must have been such a relief.'

'Yes, a relief for my family. But what about all the other false-positives who were never told about the need for an additional confirmatory test? That really bothered me. Hence that letter.'

'What happened when you gave the letter?'

'Long story . . . there was an argument . . . and I lost my job.'

The office was relatively empty when Amit returned after the long weekend. Several people were away on their summer break. He could see Addy hammering away at her laptop in her cubicle and decided that he would take her out for coffee and tell her everything. Even as he was taking out the registers from his bag and placing them on his desk, the office peon came up and told him that Mrs Rudra wanted to see him immediately.

She sat behind her large desk, as intimidating as ever with her large red bindi and kohl-lined eyes. The wall behind her was full of photographs showing her with various luminaries, including a former American President and a technology billionaire famed for his global philanthropy.

'Come in and sit. I hear you have been working hard, even taking work home. May I have a look at the draft of the proposal? But, before you start, let me remind you that staff, especially temporary staff, are forbidden from taking our files outside the office.'

Amit knew from the tone of her voice that this would be a difficult conversation. As calmly as he could, he explained the problem that he had encountered.

'So, what do you propose we do?'

'Before we put in the new proposal, at the very least, we need to do a second round of confirmation tests in Nadia. We should also be careful about the claims made for Vaishali.'

'You know very well that the deadline is approaching and we do not have the time to send the team out again.'

'Then you should be aware that we will be grossly misrepresenting the HIV situation in Nadia and basically lying about what was achieved in Vaishali.'

'Mr Menon, I hope you know who you are talking to . . . I don't need to be taught what is appropriate and what is inappropriate by a child like you. You see all those awards along the wall? I did not get them for nothing. Do you know how many government committees I serve on? If you think we are lying, it is best that you leave this office immediately. And yes, do return the registers that you stole from us.'

Amit realized that there was no point arguing. He got up and went directly to his desk, put his personal items into his bag and walked out. He did not even stop by Addy's desk to say goodbye. He went down to the cafe and ordered himself a double espresso and a sandwich. He had been sitting there dazed for half an hour when Addy called on the mobile and asked him where he was. She came down to the cafe with her friend Mala in tow.

'I just heard that you had a big fight with Mrs Rudra and walked out . . . You've got to be better behaved when dealing with a senior, respected person like her.'

'Well, I did not walk out, I was kicked out. And, I was merely trying to do my job . . .'

For the second time that day, Amit explained his findings.

'I understand what you mean, Amit, but we need this US$2 million and the deadline is close. We simply don't have the time to redo the survey. Just come back and apologize to Mrs Rudra and finish the proposal . . . I will talk to her and request her to take you back.'

'I agree with Addy. Besides, all the money is for doing good, isn't it? Why are you getting so carried away by some statistics? All projects have such problems, should we stop doing them?'

'But, how can you ignore . . .'

'I don't know what has happened to you in the last few weeks. You have been repeatedly rude to my friends and now you have gone and fought with my boss—after all my effort to find you a proper job . . . you could have easily converted this into a regular job with us after we received the funds.'

'You will turn Addy into a laughing stock when everyone hears about this . . . after all the things she has done for you.'

'Really, if you don't come back right now and apologize to Mrs Rudra, I will never speak to you again.'

Amit had heard similar arguments before—on conference calls with London and New York. He got up, paid the bill and left.

He stood in the blazing summer sun. The world seemed to dance around him. It was the same feeling that he had had that Friday evening in Singapore. He needed to get out.

A week later, the former bond trader found himself back in Nubra Valley. He sat near the wooden footbridge, his legs in the sun and his head in the shade of a tree, reading Ryszard Kapuscinski's *Travels with Herodotus*. There were two beers chilling in the stream. At some point he became aware that someone was standing near him. He looked up. It was a young woman, medium height, wearing a black pullover.

'Hi, are you here on a holiday?'

'You could say that . . .'

'I am here working for an NGO; we work on women's issues. I have to write a report on a project we are doing here.'

'I wish you luck.'

And then, Amit turned to his book and continued reading.

The Reunion

Dev heaved a sigh of relief as Starlight Express crossed the line, a hair's breadth ahead of the favourite. He had recouped the day's losses and was up a modest sum. Not bad for a last-minute pick. It was the last race, and the screams and cheers died down as people began to shuffle out. Dev walked to the counter behind the Victorian-era stands to collect his winnings. It was relatively empty— few others had bet on Starlight. He had been a regular here for more than two decades and the lady at the counter acknowledged him with a slight nod as she counted out the notes. Along with the last of the crowd, Dev made his way out to the road. The traffic was heavy and, just outside the gates, there was a throng trying to flag taxis down—futile at this time of the day.

He made his way across the bridge and waited near the hotel. It was the best spot, he had gathered from long experience. Sure enough, he got a cab within a few minutes. Just in time too. The clouds had been building up and it soon began to rain. The traffic became even slower.

People stood under any shelter they could find—bus stops, large trees and the porches of office buildings. The tired expressions of those who have worked all day and just want to go home.

It took almost half an hour to get to Park Street. The rain had eased to a light drizzle. The taxi stopped in front of Oxford Bookstore. Dev stepped over a few puddles to the corner stall and bought himself a cigarette. He lit it with the smouldering coir and then smoked it leisurely. He muttered a few pleasantries to the occasional familiar face that drifted past him.

By the time he made it next door to Olypub, it was dark outside. Inside, the regulars had by now taken their usual places. His table had been left free. He nodded at a few people as he walked to it. He knew only some of their names but he saw them every week—first at the races and then at Oly. The waiter did not come to take his order, he appeared within a few minutes with a large peg of Old Monk with ice and a bottle of cola. Dev leisurely poured the cola into the rum, and took a long sip. A complimentary plate of masala peanuts came as usual. The conversation around him was heating up and he leaned back, waiting.

It was another half an hour before Bhaskar arrived. Medium height, a bit over forty, the confident gait of a sportsman. He was in a white linen shirt and black trousers, but gave the impression of being somewhat overdressed for Oly. Bhaskar stood at the door and looked uncertainly at the once familiar scene. The wooden tables, the faux-leather seats, the large smoke-stained mirrors, the waiters in faded white. He slowly surveyed the faces till his attention was drawn to a man waving at him from the back.

'Hello, Dev. Thanks for waving out, I wouldn't have recognized you. It's been a long time!'

'It has been a long time indeed. Don't blame you for failing to recognize me—the moustache, all the grey hair, the pot belly. Besides, I have the advantage of regularly seeing you on TV and in the magazines.'

'It was such a wonderful surprise to get your call this morning. I have been wondering where you disappeared. I have been regularly exchanging emails with Abhi, Anita and Mihir but none of them knew where to find you. I even did a Google search for you but came up with nothing. How did you know where I was staying?'

'I read in the papers that you were in town—then I called all the likely hotels. Not so difficult. Anyway, it's good to see you in person after all these years. What's it been? Twenty-three years?'

'Yes, twenty-three years. I have not seen you since that summer I left for university. In fact, I last met you right here at Oly on the evening before I took the flight out.'

'Yes it was here—I remember that summer clearly. All that rum and beer, the hours of debating and dreaming.

Luckily that was before they enforced the minimum age for drinking. Say, should I order a drink for you?'

'Old Monk and cola—still my favourite. So, tell me, what have you been up to?'

'I work as an accountant at a small trading house called Spencer, Baksh & Co. One of those old British-era companies, but now owned by a Marwari businessman. I have been there since I finished my BCom. Light work and plenty of free time. I spend it writing fiction for sundry magazines, and then I am a bit of a Turf Club addict.'

'Isn't everybody at Oly's? I rarely have the time these days, unfortunately. But, remember how Shankar used to place the bets for all of us because he was the only one who didn't look underage? Also, remember how you won a thousand rupees on a single bet—a lot of money for us in those days! I even remember the name of the horse— Silver Ghost or something like that.'

'Yes, it was Silver Ghost. The win funded several days of feasting on seekh kebabs and chicken rolls at the old dhaba.'

'Is the old dhaba still there?'

'Yes, but it has been all dolled up into a middle-class restaurant. The kebabs have really gone downhill.'

The rum and cola arrived, accompanied with a bowl with ice and a dish heaped with chanachur. Bhaskar sank back into the chair and looked at the scene reflected in the large mirror. It brought back a rush of memories and emotions. The bar was now full of chatter, the clinking of glasses and bottles. Someone behind the pillar sang two lines of Manna Dey.

'It's good to be back, Dev.'

'Hope you will visit us more often now.'

'Now tell me about the family. Do you have kids? I assume you married Paromita . . .'

'No, I did not. Don't look so surprised—we broke up many years ago—barely a year or two after I graduated. She went off to Bombay to study fashion design and to try her luck in Bollywood and modelling. She wanted me to shift to Bombay but I refused. To cut a long story short, there was a hell of a row and then we went our own ways.'

'Don't tell me! I cannot believe it! The two of you were such a handsome couple. We all thought you were so perfect together. Are you still in touch with her?'

'She never got anywhere in Bollywood but married a stockbroker. Two daughters. She still looks stunning.'

'So you are still in touch with her. Does she come here often?'

'Not really. The last time we exchanged letters was several years ago. She comes here very rarely—and then it's usually too hurried. However, I do visit her mother occasionally. She still lives in the old house, all alone now. She shows me all the latest photographs from Bombay, so I keep up to date.'

'So did you marry someone else?'

'No. In my late twenties I did actively want to get married but somehow didn't meet anyone. Now I am quite content with Olypub and the Turf Club—not good places to find a suitable bride, I'm afraid. Who knows, I may yet find the right girl . . .'

'Are you in touch with any of the others from school?'

'You seem to be in touch with more people than I am. Most of you left town for various jobs and universities and no one really came back, not from our gang anyway. I heard that Shankar is a techie in Bangalore, Rishi is somewhere in the US and Aditi is a businesswoman in Hyderabad. I have not heard from them in years—my fault really, I am quite poor with email. Don't even have a Facebook account.'

'And where do you live now? The old bungalow on Southern Avenue?'

'We sold the old bungalow a decade ago when my brother's family moved to Gurgaon. It was just too big for me anyway. I now stay in an apartment that I inherited from an uncle—it's just twenty minutes from here by metro; very convenient. But enough about me, let's talk about you. You have done so well, I am really proud of you.'

'I owe it to you. If you remember, all the others had a choice of alternatives and contingency plans, but not me. I have had a number of lucky breaks in my life, but that one I owe to you.'

'I know your wife's name is Suchitra. How did you meet her?'

'Believe it or not, I met her on the flight out to Heathrow. She was going to Cambridge and she sat next to me on the flight. We got chatting—and kept up a correspondence through the university years. I suppose we were both lonely in a foreign country. Then she found a job in Hong Kong. I followed her there and we got married. We were there for three years and then I did my MBA. I had no income and she had to support me for those years. Then I got a good break in the software industry. The rest you know from the papers.'

'I would love to meet her.'

'You will. She will be picking me up for dinner. Should be here any minute now. Hope she finds this place. I drew her a map but she is really poor with directions. Hope she is carrying her mobile phone.'

'Another Old Monk?'

'Yes. And some more chanachur.'

'There is a matter that I would prefer to discuss before your wife arrives. I need a favour from you. Feel free to refuse but I can think of no one else to turn to.'

'Tell me. Of course I will do my best.'

'I need a loan of about Rs 4 lakh. I have some debts. Had a bad run at the races last year and foolishly turned to a loan shark. The interest rate is steep and I cannot really keep up with the payments. Now the moneylender wants the principal back and has become somewhat aggressive in recent months. The apartment is already mortgaged, and I am reluctant to ask my company for any more help. As I said, feel free to refuse.'

'The money is not a problem. Is this man threatening you with physical violence? I can speak to the chief minister.'

'The money is enough to buy my freedom. Leave the chief minister out, I do not want to escalate this.'

'Suchi usually has our chequebook in her handbag . . . and that's her at the door.'

Suchitra stepped inside. She was in a simple sari but, like her husband, somehow gave the impression of being overdressed for the bar. She stood there blinking in the dim light till she located her husband at the back.

'You must be Dev. Wonderful to meet you at last. I have been looking forward to meeting you. Bhaskar keeps talking about you and your high-school exploits—how you are an excellent singer, how you were the state tennis champion, how you were a maths whiz, how you had the best-looking girlfriend in the city.'

'All exaggerations, I assure you. Please do sit down. May I order a drink for you?'

'Thanks, but we are in a bit of a hurry. We are already late for dinner. It's raining again and the traffic is really bad. Why not lunch tomorrow? Bhaskar has some meetings but I may be free. We can talk at leisure then.'

'I will call you in the morning to confirm a time and place. Let me take you out for lunch and then a tour of our old school. Perhaps Bhaskar can join us after his meetings.'

'That may well work but let me confirm this tomorrow morning. I have an aunt here and need to visit her as well.'

'Suchi, could you give me the chequebook? I need to give Dev some money.'

'Already doing business deals, I see . . .'

'Not quite. What's the date?'

Bhaskar made out a cheque for Rs 4,00,000 and handed it to Dev. He then settled the bar bill and walked out into the night with his wife.

'So that was the famous Dev. Must say, I am rather disappointed—he is certainly not very impressive at first glance. Looks more like an unshaven drunk, and at least a decade older than you.'

'He has aged quite a lot; I could barely recognize him. But, you should have seen him at eighteen. The way he sang, the way he played tennis, the way he looked in the school captain's uniform. All of us hero worshipped him.'

'What about his gorgeous wife? To you she was the most beautiful woman alive. All teenage hormones, I think.'

'I just found out that they did not get married. I was quite taken aback although I am not sure why . . . It was a long time ago and things do not always turn out the way one imagines. It was just something embedded in my head for so long.'

'And the cheque? What was that about?'

'He needed the money for something. He is already in debt and there is no one else he can turn to.'

'And you simply gave it to him! It's quite a large sum to hand to an old drunk just because you knew him in school.'

'Let's say it's an old debt I had to repay.'

'That explains why he contacted you after all these years.'

'Suchi, please let this matter be . . . We can easily afford it . . . I do not want to discuss it any further.'

'It's your money, you are free to give it to anyone.'

'No need to be sarcastic. I know he will probably never give it back . . . but if he had not turned down the scholarship, I would not have been on that flight where I first met you . . .'

～

Dev waited for his old friend to walk out of the pub. He reread the cheque, folded it carefully and slipped it into his shirt pocket. Then, he took his glass and strolled over to a table where three of the regulars sat sipping whisky and soda.

'Come, Dev. We have been waiting to hear you sing. How about a long session of Hemanta tonight?'

'Tonight is good for a long session. But first, you must give me a few good tips for next week's Derby. It's been over a year since I last had the money to play for proper stakes.'

The Caretaker

On a blazing summer's day, government officials from the City came and erected four pillars on the four corners of a plot of land. The plot was on a low, barren hill that overlooked the Village. It was not far from the village temple and the adjoining primary school, but only the goatherds frequented the place. The hill was classified in official documents as 'forest land' but the woodcutters had done away with the trees long ago and the goats had stripped the hill of the remaining vegetation; only the sturdiest thorn-bushes had survived. The sun beat down on its dusty, eroded slopes.

We, the villagers, stared at the new pillars with wonder. No one had told us their purpose. Certainly the government surveyors and officials were too busy to be asked. Some of the peasants grumbled that the City people were usurping land that had belonged to the Village for generations. Others, more hopeful, speculated that this was at last the village clinic that had long been promised by the government.

A few weeks later, construction workers arrived. Tents were set up to house them. Then arrived the large earth movers and bulldozers. Later came the bricks, the cement mixer, the steel rods. A tea stall appeared, complete with a radio that belted out old favourites and cricket commentary. The place was abuzz with a gaggle of contractors and construction workers. Work proceeded at a furious pace for the next ten months. The village prostitute grew conspicuously prosperous and expanded her establishment.

When the village elders asked the project supervisor what was being built, the man simply said that he had 'orders'. One morning, we saw a large signboard that read:

This is a project under the IRDP Scheme. Trespassers will be prosecuted.

In less than a year, there was large structure on the hill. It was three storeys high. It had a door on its west side and a single glass window facing south on the second floor. There was nothing else to disturb its perfect shape. They painted the building a flawless white that shone in the hot sun. This was the most impressive edifice in the Village. We were proud of it—it was even larger than the old temple that graced the village in the next valley.

A week after it was completed, a large number of
people in cars and buses arrived from the City. The IRDP
building was festooned with banners, and loudspeakers
blared from the corners. There was a smart podium and
a marquee filled with chairs. Cold drinks and hot snacks
were being served. There was an atmosphere of great
festivity. The villagers were not invited but some of us
sat further up the slope and watched all this with interest.

At midday, arrived a black car from which stepped
a man dressed as flawlessly in white as the edifice itself.
He was clearly a very important man, and we were later
told that he was a cabinet minister. The minister planted
a sapling in front of the main door. Then he made a
passionate speech about how the nation was stepping
forward into the future, how future generations would
look back at 'our' valiant efforts to develop the country's
economy. The crowds cheered. The minister pushed his
way past the photographers, got back into the black car and
left, sirens blaring. The City people got back into their cars
and buses and we watched them disappear into the dust.

My cousin, who works in the City, later told me that
the minister's speech was in the newspapers the next day
and there were even pictures of our Village. We felt proud.

A few days later, the building supervisor came to our
Village. He parked his jeep near the well and went directly
to the headman's house. The headman called a meeting
of the village council. In the shade of the old banyan tree,

the headman told the council that the government wanted to recruit someone from the Village as the caretaker for the new edifice. This was an important job. The council deliberated for hours for they had to choose someone who would bring honour to the Village. At last, they decided to nominate me as I was the only literate boy in the Village who had not left for the City. I was twenty and I was pleased.

I reported at the IRDP building the next morning. The supervisor and his assistant listed out my tasks. I was to look after the structure and prevent anyone from entering it, except of course IRDP staff. It did not yet have an electric connection but, I was assured, it would be set right as soon as the engineers arrived. I was also expected to tend to the grounds and water the sapling planted by the minister. There was no water supply yet, but that too would be set right when the engineers arrived. For now, I would have to bring a bucket of water up from the village well. I was also told that the second floor had a window, and that I should never open it. For all this work, the government would pay me Rs 350 a month.

They asked me if I had any questions. I asked them the purpose of the construction. They said that they were following 'orders'. I asked them when the engineers would arrive. They said that it was none of their business. Then they handed me the keys and left in the jeep.

I was now the possessor of The Keys. How the village boys would envy me. How they would beg me to allow them in. But I would never give in. I had a responsibility given to me by the government and to the nation. It was a matter of honour and duty. I unlocked the door and stepped in. It was pitch-dark inside even at midday.

I returned the next day with a candle. The ground floor was a maze of corridors. It was several days before I could confidently make my way through the labyrinth. At the far corner was a flight of stairs that led to the first floor. It was as dark as the ground floor and consisted of a series of empty cells, some with doors and others without. Most of the cells were square but three were triangular and one was semicircular. Another flight of stairs led to the second floor—a large hall with the sun streaming in through the solitary window. To eyes now used to darkness, the light appeared almost obscene. On the wall opposite the window was a large sign that read:

This Is an IRDP Project: Helping Grow the Nation

I could not fathom the purpose of my charge but I was awed by the mysterious geometry. I swept clean each floor twice a week. The door was firmly shut for the rest of the time. The sapling posed more of a problem. The village-goats took to eating its tender leaves. I shooed them away several times but they always came back. I quarrelled with the goatherds who stopped talking to me but did not stop their goats. They told me that the government job had gone to my head. I tried to create a rough fencing with thorn-bushes but it did not work. At last, out of exasperation, I decided to write to the authorities to request for a fence and barbed wire.

I wrote: 'I am the Caretaker of the IRDP building built by the government last year near the village of Rupmar.' I hoped this made sense to them. I had considered a more detailed description such as 'The building is white and was built on a hill that overlooks the village from the south-east. It has three floors. The first floor has a labyrinth, the second a series of small rooms and the last one a window.' In the end, I did not send the detailed description for fear that I would appear foolish to them. The government must already know all about my building. They had the original architect's plans. Probably there were detailed reports about its place in the workings of the world. The engineers were surely devising elaborate plans for it. So I merely asked for some barbed wire to protect the sapling.

I wrote to them many times, but never received a reply. Finally, I devised a sturdy fence of wooden stakes and stone but it was too late. The sapling died. I was now afraid that the engineers would scold me when they arrived and perhaps even throw me out of my job. I would, of course, tell them that I had written to the government asking for barbed wire but they may not believe me. I would be shamed in front of my village. Perhaps the minister would have to come back and plant another sapling. The whole country would hold me accountable for letting them down.

Therefore, it is quite fortunate that the engineers never came.

~

Thirty years have now passed. My son works in the City and my daughter now lives in the next village with her husband. I still clean the three floors, but the white paint has become a dull grey and is peeling. Some of the window panes broke two years ago. I suspect one of the village boys—his father always envied my official position. Now, during the monsoon season, rainwater flows down the stairs and floods the labyrinth. Despite my best efforts, the damp is encouraging mould on the walls. I have sent a detailed report to the government. They have not replied. Perhaps the cost of repair cannot be justified. Perhaps it fulfils the purpose of the labyrinth. I have no complaints about my job except that my salary of Rs 350 buys little these days. My wife is frequently unwell and needs medicines. My children have their own lives and families, and I do not wish to be a burden on them.

Last month I wrote again, asking for a raise. At last, I have received a reply. It reads thus:

To,

The Caretaker,
IRDP Building,
Rupmar

(Ref. folder number: FG/T4/73)

Sir,

This is in response to the letters we have received
from you requesting an increase in your monthly
remuneration. After carefully reviewing all the letters
(filed under above-mentioned folder), we regret to tell
you that we are not in a position to increase your salary.

We understand that the increase in the Consumer
Price Index (Rural Non-Agricultural) would
have eroded the purchasing power of your salary.
Unfortunately, the Integrated Rural Development
Programme (IRDP) was discontinued twenty-seven
years and four months ago and was replaced by the
Comprehensive Rural Development Plan (CRDP).
Eleven years ago, this too was replaced by the
Accelerated Rural Development Mission (ARDM).
Therefore, we no longer require your services.

However, in view of your long service, we have
agreed to give you a lifelong pension of Rs 227.42 per

month. This will be wired to you as before on the first Monday of every month. As a special consideration, we will recommend that the amount be reviewed by the next Public Sector Pay Commission (PSPC) in five years' time.

Regards,

S.D. Kumar
Section Officer (Grade 2)
Payments and Personnel Department
Room 51 R
Ministry of Rural Welfare

Before You Judge Me

When you have climbed the same mountain,
When you have felt the pain of my broken toes,
When you have cut through impenetrable jungles
And bled from my open sores.

When you have stumbled in my darkness,
When you have stood in the rising flood,
When you've been swept away by the cold waters
That have frozen your very blood.

Then, and only then, may you judge me.
You may think me good or evil,
Or perhaps a mere fool
But I know, more likely than not, you will forgive me.

The Conference Call

All hell broke loose in the accounts department when the telecom company presented a bill of a few million dollars for an international conference call that had gone on for three months. The head of the accounts department wrote back indignantly saying that the bill was obviously untenable because no conference call could go on for that long. The telecom company reverted with incontrovertible proof that the conference call had indeed taken place, including a full recording of the proceedings. A subsequent investigation revealed what had transpired.

It all began when a college dropout set up a company called Call-Con in his basement and developed an app that could stand in for people who had to attend long and tedious conference calls. The attendee had to call into the conference call and say a few initial pleasantries to establish his/her presence, but could then leave the app to handle the rest once the Senior Company Bore began his monologue. The app user would have prerecorded in their own voice a few set phrases such as 'Interesting, please go on', 'Can you repeat the last bit, please', 'This may be a possible solution but have you discussed it with legal and compliance' and so on. Artificial intelligence recognized gaps in the conversation and inserted these phrases appropriately into the discussion. As an additional precaution, the app was also able to recognize when a specific question was aimed at the user and would then play back 'Let me look into this and get back to you next week'. A short recording of the question was then sent to the user for further action.

The app became very popular and went viral within months. Although no one admitted to using it, a technology magazine estimated that 30–40 per cent of conference call attendees worldwide were using the app part or all of the time. In fact, there was many an occasion when virtually all of the attendees on a conference call, with the exception of the Senior Company Bore, were being proxied by the app. The senior company bores, oddly, did not seem to have noticed the difference. Even those bores who had heard of the app were smug in the belief that no one would ever dream of using it on them.

Two years later, Call-Con was listed on the New York Stock Exchange at an initial valuation of over a billion dollars. At the celebratory dinner, the founder made a passionate speech about how his company was 'making the world a better place'. For once, many people genuinely agreed. One of the attendees begged him to work on an application that would automatically wish people Happy Birthday on social media and 'like' all photographs of pets that their friends posted. This was sure to improve social harmony and promote world peace. The suggestion received loud applause.

A professor of English literature from a well-known university wrote a long newspaper article highlighting the absurdity of the situation and argued passionately that nothing better could be expected from the crass commercialization of the art of conversation by business schools and the technology industry. He soon set up a Society for the Preservation of Conference Calls at his university and several passionate student activists joined it. They held violent protests that succeeded in cancelling a university lecture by the founder of Call-Con. The professor was, however, conspicuously silent when the company announced a few months later that it was releasing an app that could spontaneously generate scholarly reviews of works of art, fine wines and high literature. A few of his rivals subsequently did point out a noticeable increase in the frequency of his publications in high-brow journals.

So, what did the investigation uncover about the multimillion-dollar con-call bill? It seems that everyone on the call had been using the app that day but the Senior Company Bore had somehow failed to call in. Since no one delivered a monologue, the app was unable to discern when the call ended. The discussion kept running with the app inserting prerecorded phrases from different attendees to keep the conversation going. The conference call went on for three full months till, luckily, someone in the telecom company noticed something was wrong and considerately ended the call.

The possibility of such a situation had occurred to some of the programmers at Call-Con while developing the software, but they had concluded that it was impossible, even with all the latest artificial intelligence, for a mere programme to discern if a conference call was dead or alive. The glitch, therefore, could not be corrected. They need not have worried. Neither the users nor the telecom companies ever raised the matter.

As for the multimillion-dollar bill—it was quietly settled. Many senior executives had been involved and no one wanted to attract attention to it. The bill was classified under 'Other Miscellaneous Business Expenses' when company accounts were next presented to shareholders. There were furious debates on a number of issues at the shareholders' meet but no one noticed the spike in an innocuous category at the bottom of the page. The Senior Company Bore who had failed to call in, however, was not so lucky. He was replaced for dereliction of duty.

The Intellectuals

The yellow Ambassador taxi rattled to a halt by the side of the street. It was hot, humid and crowded with pedestrians, hawkers and vehicles of all description. Stalls of second-hand books, their wares piled high, seemed to spill over from the footpath on to the road. Holly looked around from inside the taxi and decided that it was the right place. She paid the driver without haggling, even though she was sure that she had been overcharged. Then she stepped into the sun and the noisy bustle.

Bored hawkers turned to look at her with curiosity. It was not that they were unused to seeing a white foreigner walking down this street. A couple of them drifted through every week but they were usually backpackers and occasionally exchange students—wandering around trying to get the 'authentic experience' as promised by their guidebooks. For some reason they always looked scruffy and dressed in the peculiar loose, cotton tie-and-dye that a certain class of backpackers believes makes them look like they have 'been out there'. Even more inexplicably, some of them sported a checked, Palestinian keffiyeh wrapped around their neck like a scarf—entirely unsuitable for the humidity of a Bengali summer—as if the piece of cloth somehow signalled their solidarity with the sufferings of all of the Third World.

Holly, however, was dressed in a light business suit and her hair was neatly set. She gave the impression of a corporate professional. She scanned the decaying colonial-era buildings that hovered over the street and tried to guess which one housed the Coffee House. Finally she walked over to a tea-stall owner and asked for directions.

The entrance to the building was somewhat different from what Holly had expected. She had heard about how the Coffee House was the intellectual epicentre of the city but the stairwell she now found herself in was crumbling and was half blocked by an old scooter and flanked on one side by a wall of exposed electrical wires. There were people going in and coming out, so Holly decided to take her chances and walk up the stairs. One floor up, she found herself in a large hall with a high ceiling. Rows of tables filled the hall even as hanging ceiling fans stirred the sultry air. There were many people sitting about drinking tea or coffee, chatting and arguing amid the tinkle of spoons stirring sugar in ceramic cups, while an imposing portrait of the Great Poet looked down at the scene from a peeling yellow wall. The place had clearly seen better days.

Holly wondered how she would identify her contact person as she scanned the room. She had just arrived in the city the previous day and had only ever exchanged emails with him. Fortunately, someone waved to her from across the hall and walked up to her.

'Dr Holly Katz?'

'Yes, and I presume you are Biplab Mullick.'

'Hope you did not have trouble finding Coffee House. Everyone knows it.'

'No problem at all. And thank you for arranging this meeting with your group of eminent intellectuals.'

'Best minds in the country, madam. We have been meeting here twice a week for the last thirty-five years. Real thinkers, not like the shallow fellows in Delhi, arguing loudly on television every night.'

Biplab led Holly to a table where five others were sitting. Four men and a woman, in their sixties, with greying hair. All the men were in half-sleeved, checked shirts, untucked, and leather sandals. The lady was in a cotton sari with a fading brown-and-grey pattern, her oily hair tied tightly in a neat bun. On the table were several half-drunk cups of tea and coffee as well as books and newspapers in Bengali and English. Holly quickly surmised that the leader of the group was the man sitting directly under the portrait of the Great Poet. While the others sat on cheap plastic chairs, he sat on a large wooden one that had probably survived from the colonial era.

A tall man with a pot belly that pushed against his loose shirt. He sat with an air of detached authority, a confident smirk under his thick-framed glasses.

'Let me introduce you first to Dr Surojit Haldar. He used to teach postcolonial literature at DK College, and writes regularly on important national and international matters. Just before you arrived, we were discussing his latest column on sports policy . . . He was very close to the previous chief minister but the government changed. Otherwise he would have been the head of the department.'

Surojit nodded and smiled benevolently.

'And this is Rabin Sen. He makes documentaries and experimental art films. Very famous. Even won an international award in Prague in 1987.'

'It was Warsaw 1986,' Rabin corrected.

Biplab went on undeterred, 'And this is Asad Ali, social worker and Marxist poet. He was also an MLA in the nineties but decided to leave active politics and work full-time for the uplift of the masses. He can tell you everything about grass roots.'

'And Gayatri-di, she is a great scholar of economic geography—first class first and gold medallist in 1977. She has written a seminal paper on the cooperative movement in the brass utensils industry in eastern Midnapur district. Even Americans know her—she is a member of the National Geographic Society.'

Holly wanted to say that anyone who subscribed to the *National Geographic* magazine was called a member but she held her tongue. Nevertheless, the woman in the sari would maintain a cold distance throughout Holly's stay in the city.

'And, as you know, I was a journalist but am currently editing a book on the dialectic materialism embedded in the works of nineteenth-century poet Michael Madhusudan Dutta.'

With that Biplab sat down. Holly noticed that he had left out the small, mousy man at the end of the table. She would later learn that he was Subho Maitra, a clerk in the weights and measures department, and a camp follower. He was a bit younger, perhaps in his early fifties, and held the others in awe. The rest did not quite treat him as an equal and made fun of him behind his back, sometimes even to his face. Subho tolerated this without complaint. Holly found that he attended all meetings religiously and read all articles, columns and poems written by the others. Indeed, he seemed to live in order to be a part of the group.

'So, you are from America? Where in America?'

'I am with the University of New Haven—I both teach and conduct research there.'

'I have been to America . . . twice. Once in 1989 to present a paper on postcolonial linguistic resonance at the University of East Texas. And then in 1995 to attend a conference organized by my friend Savitri Biwaque. Do you know her?'

'I am afraid not. The US is a big place.'

'Big houses, big cars but no culture, no soul.'

'I have never been to America, but I have been to Britain. I went with an MLA delegation to attend a human rights workshop. But I have been to Dubai many times.'

'So, what brings you to Kolkata?'

'I am doing some research on Indian intellectual life and was told to come here. An Indian colleague connected me to Biplab.'

'You have come to the right place. We are not money-minded like the Gujaratis and Marwaris. Even if Kolkata has fallen behind a little in economic terms, this is still the intellectual and cultural capital of India.'

'What Bengal thinks today, India thinks tomorrow.'

In the course of the next hour and a half, over more cups of tea, the conversation took many twists and turns. A detailed comparison of Obama's position in Afghanistan versus Nixon's in Vietnam, and the nineteenth-century British experience with the Afghan Wars. From a dissection of Trump's options in the Korean Peninsula to the emerging trends in Kolkata's student politics. It then turned to an animated discussion on the general deterioration in cinematic standards due to the commercial influence of Bollywood. There was a general consensus that black-and-white European art films of the fifties represented the pinnacle of lensmanship although, of course, there was the genius of Ray.

Furious debate raged on the relative abilities of erstwhile cricket captains Mahendra Singh Dhoni, Sourav Ganguly, Lala Amarnath and Tiger Pataudi, before it turned to the relative merits of the Latin American and European styles of playing football, and whether or not Federer is really the greatest tennis player of all time. Statistics and counter-statistics were thrown about. Holly was impressed by the learned discussion but would have been even more so if she had known that none of the participants had ever actually played cricket, tennis or football.

'All this T20 cricket is not really cricket, it is entertainment. It does not show the true art. Only moneymaking.'

'Totally agree. Don't know why there is such a fuss over Kohli. Wouldn't have lasted long against the West Indies bowling attack of the 1970s. Totally failed . . .'

'I was in Eden all five days during the Test of December 1978, when Gavaskar scored 107 before being caught by Bacchus off Philip in the first innings. He then went on to score 182 not out in the second.'

'The crowds used to understand Test cricket in those days. Not like now . . . just want a spectacle.'

Subho listened intently to the conversation and jotted down the significant observations in a small notebook.

He occasionally ventured a comment but was mostly ignored.

Holly stayed in Kolkata for several more weeks and met the group many times. They initially met at the Coffee House but the American academic tired of the place and the oily snacks, and managed to convince the others to have their gatherings at bars and cafes in and around Park Street. The intellectuals were somewhat reluctant to shift on the principle that these places were elitist but readily agreed when Holly made it clear that she would pay all the bills. Eventually she invited them to Calcutta Club—a centrally located colonial-era club that she could access through a reciprocal arrangement.

It was while sipping Makaibari tea in the Calcutta Club veranda that Holly told the others that her university was organizing a conference on postcolonial literary theory and was inviting papers from leading experts. They would be very pleased to accept a submission from India.

'Surojit-da is the obvious person to do this. He would have been head of department if the government had not changed.'

Dr Surojit Haldar smiled nonchalantly. 'I am very busy these days, but I will see what I can do to help you with this.'

'That would be wonderful. We will pay for all travel expenses, of course, and make arrangements for your stay in New Haven for the duration of the conference . . . The only hitch is that the submission date is just two months away.'

'I had submitted a paper to Prof. Daniel Nelson of Harvard in 1997 for his quarterly journal. He had replied to me that they would get back after carefully examining the paper. I will show you the letter. But they have still not got back. Probably the fellow is still trying to understand the section where I had validated my thesis on Derrida. Anyway, I will not wait for Harvard any longer and will send you an updated version . . .'

'Please send it to us and I am sure the conference organizers would love to hear you speak about it.'

'I also want to submit a paper.'

Everyone turned to look at Subho. This was possibly the first time ever that he was enjoying the full attention of the group.

After a short silence, Surojit smiled patronizingly. 'Yes, Subho, you must.'

Holly returned to New Haven a few days later. Seven weeks later, she received two papers in her inbox: 'A Formal Deconstruction of Tagore's Narratives within an Alta-Derridean Epistemological Darstellung' by Dr Surojit Haldar and 'A Multi-Step Teleological Examination of Subaltern Literary Heuristics in Post-Colonial Bengal' by Subhojit Maitra.

A couple of weeks later, the office of Prof. Holly Katz sent out an airline ticket and a formal invitation letter to

Mr Subhojit Maitra requesting him to present his paper at the University of New Haven. A separate letter was sent to Dr Haldar thanking him for his submission and assuring him that the paper would be given due consideration for future events.

Holly personally drove down to Newark to pick up Subho and made sure he had a comfortable room at the visiting faculty block. The conference was not a large affair—around thirty-five students and a handful of faculty members. Two doctoral candidates presented their papers, followed by Subho. He wore his best suit and a borrowed yellow tie. The audience asked a few polite questions and it was over. Holly made sure she took several photographs of Subho as he spoke and later a group photograph together with the audience. The following day, Holly drove him back to the airport. On the way, she made a detour to show him Manhattan. Subho was very pleased and thanked the professor profusely.

~

A few months later, a yellow Ambassador taxi rattled to a halt by the side of the crowded street. The taxi-driver quoted an inflated fare but Holly handed him the correct amount and got off before the driver could argue. One of the bookstall owners gave her a nod of recognition as she confidently made her way to the Coffee House.

She found her group of intellectuals in deep discussion at their usual table. The same people were there but their seating arrangement had changed. Subho now sat on the colonial-era wooden chair, directly under the portrait of the Great Poet. The others were listening intently as he made a strong case for the regulation of soap advertising, when he looked up and saw Holly making her way across the hall. He gave her a benevolent smile.

~

No more than a year had passed when the following article appeared in the *Quarterly Journal of Social Anthropology*:

A Study of Intellectual Hierarchies in Stagnation
Author: Prof. Holly Katz, University of New Haven

The author would like to thank the John and Sally Depp Foundation for their generous funding of this project. She is also grateful to the faculty and students of the School of Social Anthropology for organizing the mock conference that was critical for the study.

Abstract
This is a study of group dynamics in the context of intellectual stagnation. Given the overall context of stagnation, the hierarchy within the group can remain

frozen for very long periods of time. However, in a controlled experiment, we found that group dynamics can still be manipulated through external stimulus. This is possible because the incumbent hierarchy is itself based on claims of external validation since prolonged stagnation precludes internal validation. Thus, changing the relative claims of external validation can radically overturn the hierarchy of such a group of intellectuals. The paper contains the full record of the experiment conducted over 2017–18 but the names of mentioned individuals have been deliberately changed in order to protect their identities.

Waiting at the Time of
Cow-Dust

Subhadra sat in front of her hut cutting a few meagre vegetables for the evening meal. The low sun threw long shadows over the wooded hills. From her vantage on top of the ridge, she could see the rest of the village below. Smoke was rising slowly from some of the huts as evening fires were being lit. The twitter of birds heading home, the laughter of children playing and the distant tinkle of bells as the herds returned from the day's grazing. But Subhadra's eyes were searching the narrow path that wound along the hills and into the next valley.

The previous day, a platoon of government soldiers had come to the village. The platoon commander had knocked on the door and asked for her husband. Subhadra had seen the captain a few times before. Her husband was not just the village headman but also knew these parts better than anyone else. He was also a crack shot. His grandfather had been the game warden of a local nobleman before the republic had been established. So, he had inherited a couple of excellent rifles and an intimate

knowledge of the surrounding hills and valleys. Although
the big game was now protected, he still indulged in
hunting small game to supplement the meagre produce of
the land and the little he earned occasionally from being a
guide for visiting government officials.

Nevertheless, Subhadra was always apprehensive
when her husband accompanied soldiers for she knew
they were making raids on rebel guerrilla camps. He
never spoke about the trips but she knew that it was not
just for the money. He had always been suspicious of the
rebels' cause and this antipathy had grown after the rebels
had forcibly taken away two young girls from the village
ten years earlier. No one had heard from the girls again
but the village had banded together. Under the leadership
of Subhadra's husband, the rebels had not been allowed
to establish their influence in the surrounding area and
had been forced to move further south.

Her husband, however, was not at home when the
soldiers had arrived the previous morning. He and some
of the menfolk had gone to the state capital, three days'
journey away, to deliver a petition. The commander was a
bit upset to hear this. He explained that they had reliable
information that a very important rebel leader was camping
half a day's march away. They had been searching for him
for years. This was a big opportunity but they needed
someone who knew the terrain intimately. On hearing
that their guide was unavailable, the commander went

back to his men and they stood about muttering among themselves and wondering what to do next. The captain then returned to the hut to ask if there was anyone else in the village who could help them.

It was then that Subhadra's sixteen-year-old son offered to guide the soldiers. The mother was vehemently against this. After all, he was no more than a boy. The son insisted that he wanted to go. He argued that he was now a man, that his father had frequently taken him hunting in that same valley, that he knew all the watering holes and caves in the area. For almost an hour the two argued but Subhadra would not relent. The captain assured the mother that his soldiers would take good care of the teenager and protect him with their lives. So eventually, and very reluctantly, she agreed to let her son go. Now she was waiting in front of her hut, hoping the boy would be back before dark.

A group of men became visible walking up the path in the distance. Subhadra immediately stood up and walked to the edge of the ridge to get a better look. They were still quite far away and, in the alternating light and shadow of the sunset, she could not discern which of them was her son. She did not care if they had found the rebel guerrillas, she just wanted him back home.

The story of Abhimanyu is so well known that I will spare the reader the details of what had happened.

Books

Vishwas lay on the cot, awake and not. He lazily watched the mid-morning sun stream in through the gap in the curtains and light up the books shelved all along the wall. This was the brief moment of peace in the tenement block—the children had been sent to school, the men to work and the women now sipped their tea and caught their breath after the morning frenzy. He listened to the noisy silence of a big city. The low rumble of the highway. Somewhere the news bulletin was being read over the radio. A tap was dripping.

He looked again at his beloved books and wondered how he would arrange them next. More than just reading them, he liked the feeling of owning them, holding them in his hands, re-reading the little notes he had written along the margins, rearranging them on the shelves. Sometimes he arranged them by genre, sometimes alphabetically by author but, on lonely evenings, he would often think up whimsical new ways— by the colour of their covers, alphabetically according to the last letter used in the text, by the thickness of their spines . . .

As usual, the tea-boy knocked on the door and then pushed it open. It was never locked. He left the glass of tea on the table and, without a word, ran off on his next errand. This was the signal for Vishwas to get up and start his day. He took the glass and drifted out of the door, on to the open terrace and into the bright sunshine. In an hour's time this terrace would become the hub of activity: women with their laundry, their gossip, their everyday quarrels. However, for now there was no one, the clothes lines were empty, the pigeons bobbing their heads. Two crows sat on the rusting rods of an old television antenna, a relic from another age. Vishwas sipped his tea, walked across the terrace to the basin and pulled out the razor and toothbrush hidden above the mirror.

In twenty minutes, he was shaved and washed. He quibbled with himself over the choice of clothes and then decided on an off-white shirt, ironed but not starched. Then he walked down the stairs to the lane below, past Sai Krupa General Stores, past Sai Krupa Bottles and Papers Mart and into Sai Krupa 100% Veg Restaurant. As was his custom, Vishwas chose the table nearest to the window as it afforded the best light for reading. There were many newspapers scattered about on the adjoining tables—Marathi, English, Hindi. He quickly glanced at the headlines before carefully scanning the 'Events &

Appointments' section. He made a mental note of the interesting possibilities. The tea-boy brought him his second cutting of tea, and a plate of idlis which he finished without hurry.

The train station was a short walk away. The morning rush had died down and the carriages were relatively empty. He found a good seat—no direct sun but with a good breeze. Homes, offices, trees, slums clattered by but Vishwas paid no attention. He had been doing this for eighteen years now. It seemed only yesterday that he had come to the city. He remembered his father, priest of the village temple, who supplemented his income by writing and reading letters for the illiterate. As a result, he knew better than anybody the inner lives of all the village households although he was always scrupulously discreet. He had sent his elder son Vishwas to secondary school and then on to the degree college in the nearby town.

The son performed indifferently in his studies but he was exposed to a wider world. There was a sense of freedom and movement that he had never felt before. He revelled in the anonymity. And, for the first time, he began to read. The college library had a wide variety of books and he devoured them. He wrote articles for a local magazine and spent all the earnings at the second-hand bookshop across from Palace Cinema in Civil Lines. The village now seemed too suffocating, its inhabitants too narrow. He could no longer go back there and perform the rituals of a village priest. Instead, he finished his course and headed halfway across the country to the big city.

For several years, the young man worked for a succession of small newspapers and magazines—writing articles, reporting, editing and so on. The jobs were initially steady but with the advent of the Internet, these smaller publications folded up and dissolved one after another. He tried a number of other trades—like selling washing machines to housewives—but hated them all. Vishwas eventually went back to the newspapers and became a 'freelancer'. Income was more precarious and erratic but good enough for an unattached man to rent a room in the cheaper suburbs.

In all these years he had not returned to the place of his birth. He had seen his parents but once during this time. On that occasion they had come to the city accompanied by his younger brother. He had taken them to see the usual sights—Juhu Beach, Siddhivinayak Temple and the Gateway of India. He wrote every two months and received letters and photographs in return, pictures of his brother's wife and children in their festival clothes standing stiffly in the courtyard. He had never met them and it would seem almost too embarrassing to see them in real life now. In recent years, they had occasionally spoken over his brother's mobile phone.

His parents no longer tried to coax him to marry, to have children, to 'settle down'. They had tried hard to arrange a match with the daughter of the village headmaster, an old family friend. He vaguely remembered her as a shy girl who sometimes used to watch him and the other schoolboys play cricket. Vishwas realized that she must have grown into a woman, but could not imagine spending his life with a village girl who would not understand his love of books.

Vishwas aspired to a smart city lady. He had harboured secret passions for various female colleagues at different points in time, but never had the courage to clearly articulate them. The women never seemed to take notice anyway and carried on with their lives.

The train clattered through the urban landscape. Vishwas dozed on and off. He did this often but never missed his stop. He claimed that after all these years, he could smell each railway station, and that his nose woke him up when the train was approaching his destination. He wondered if he would be able to do this after the new air-conditioned trains were introduced. He disembarked at Churchgate and walked to his usual shoeshine boy. This was his one weekly indulgence.

The boy polished the shoes.

'That will be Rs 20.'

'Twenty rupees! It was just ten a few months ago. Then you increased it to fifteen and now twenty. Surely you can do better for a regular customer like me.'

'The normal rate for this station is Rs 25, sir. What can we do, everything is becoming more expensive.'

'It's people like you who are making it expensive . . . I will pay you Rs 20 today but at this rate I will polish my own shoes from now on.'

The boy knew Vishwas did not seriously mean it, he merely argued by way of conversation. Vishwas stepped out into the sun and the bustling road—shops, hawkers, taxis, a tourist attempting to photograph decaying colonial architecture. He made his way through the familiar throng, trying to plan out the day, comparing the pros and cons of different possibilities. He lingered for a while by the second-hand bookstalls clustered near Fountain. Old copies of *National Geographic*, a complete set of the 1951 edition of Grolier's 'Lands and People' encyclopedia, a tattered copy of *Lonely Planet*'s guide to Britain. There were also bestsellers that were almost new, and pornography wrapped tightly in plastic to discourage casual browsers.

There were quite a few good bargains but he held himself back as he had only recently purchased several translated works of an obscure nineteenth-century French author and had not yet read them. Over the years, he had built up a substantial collection of books; many were shelved all along the walls of his room, more were packed in trunks under his bed along with the manuscript of a novel that he had unsuccessfully tried to publish for several years. For economy, he preferred second-hand books but had lately found that pirated versions were quite affordable as well. Vishwas was proud of his private library. They were his family. The collection would have been even larger if he still possessed the books that he had collected in his undergraduate days. He had left them in a box at his parents' home but, rather insensitively, his father had given them away when his younger brother showed no interest in them. One more reason why he had not cared to go back.

The road turned left at Regal Cinema and Vishwas followed it to the seafront promenade, and then climbed up the steps into the majestic Taj Mahal Hotel. He did not notice the fat businessmen crowding the porch, talking into their mobile phones as they waited for their cars; the short bellboy who opened the door for him; the two Arabs arguing in the lobby; the upmarket boutique displays. He came here frequently and it was all too familiar. He then walked up the grand stairwell to where the corporate functions were held.

The corporate press briefing had yet to start. The organizers were putting in last-minute finishing touches. A few other journalists had already arrived and stood around chatting over fizzies and beer. They looked very young and Vishwas did not recognize them. But the lady behind the registration counter did recognize him. She half smiled in acknowledgement and handed him the press kit.

The hotel held all manner of press briefings every day but the event managers and public relations consultants were often the same. They knew that Vishwas, like some of the other freelancers, did not work for any major publication and that they only infrequently managed to publish their articles. However, organizers usually let them into their events because they supplemented the numbers in the audience—an invaluable resource on some of the less interesting occasions. Indeed, there had been some press conferences and product launches where the audience had consisted largely of these 'regulars'.

Vishwas did not relish the corporate briefings. It was not his cup of tea—the talk about inventories and depreciation, the self-congratulatory tone of voice, the irritating young financial analysts who asked too many questions. However, he attended them religiously as they gave him a sense of being part of the mainstream. Sometimes he bumped into old acquaintances and former colleagues; sometimes they gave him a lead or a commission. Besides, the events afforded a good meal, a drink or two, often an expensive corporate gift and, in summer, a comfortable place to spend hot afternoons.

The room gradually filled up and the briefing got going, as usual, half an hour late. A tall, middle-aged man with a sheaf of papers climbed on to the podium and sat on one of the chairs. A few moments later, a younger woman walked up and sat down beside him. She was strikingly attractive. Her dark eyes shone with confidence. Her attire was formal yet showed off her trim figure. Vishwas could not take his eyes off her. He leaned towards his neighbour and whispered.

'Who is that lady, do you know?'

'Shash Dubey—she is the CEO. She's quite something, isn't she? Surely you have read about her in the biz magazines. Built the company from scratch . . .'

The audience turned silent as Ms Dubey stood up to speak. She made a few introductory remarks before embarking on a PowerPoint presentation. It was about successes and problems, earnings growth, enhancing existing distribution networks, plans for the future and revenue diversification. Vishwas did not pay attention to most of what she said. He was mesmerized by the way she spoke, her poise, the confident optimism, the flash in her eyes when she emphasized a point. Then suddenly, something on the large screen caught his attention. She was talking about corporate social responsibility and the slide showed a photograph of a village school. The company had supported the school for the past few years and had built additional classrooms, an assembly hall and a library.

It was like any other village school except perhaps the fresh coat of paint afforded by corporate support. But it looked strangely familiar to Vishwas. Apart from the new additions, he thought he could recognize the headmaster's office, with bougainvillea over the doorway. The next slide intrigued him further. On the right hand corner he could see a small temple which too looked familiar. The final photograph was of the newly built assembly hall, with the schoolchildren performing a dance drama there. The girl in the middle bore a resemblance to his niece.

Could it be his village school? He thought he could recognize some sections but others were entirely unfamiliar. It looked much larger and better maintained. The schoolchildren looked well scrubbed and in uniform, quite unlike the scruffy boys of his youth. But it had been a long time and things must have changed. In fact, the changes were the subject of the presentation. Then there was the temple, just beyond the playground. That could be a coincidence. There was nothing especially remarkable about the school or the village temple—there were probably thousands of such village schools and temples across the country. Similarly, the girl in the picture did look like his niece but he had never actually seen her in real life, only in occasional family photos sent over WhatsApp. Perhaps he could ask the attractive CEO; it would be a good excuse to engage her in conversation.

The presentation ended. There were questions and answers. Ms Dubey stepped off the podium. Vishwas had intended to catch her at this moment but she was mobbed by a group of journalists. She answered some of their questions before being whisked off by her executive assistant to an exclusive interview with one of the leading TV channels. The middle-aged man on the dais began his presentation. He was Mr Rane, finance director, and he talked about various financial details. Vishwas paid no attention. He stared out of the window at the sea and the hazy hills beyond. His mind went back to a life that he had left behind, now so far away.

He wondered what had happened to his childhood friends. He wondered about the village shopkeeper who spent most of the summer chasing away the boys from his mango trees; the Muslim classmate who wanted to be an actor but, at nineteen, went off to work in a construction site in Dubai; the headmaster's daughter whom he was asked to marry. The letters and phone conversations rarely mentioned any of them. They focused on domestic matters—the niggling illnesses of ageing parents, his brother's new motorcycle, festivals celebrated at the temple, the smartphone recently purchased by the sister-in-law. Perhaps it was time to go home and see it afresh. Of late, Vishwas had sometimes felt the urge to go home. He had always envisioned himself returning in triumph from the big city, to be fawned over by relatives and friends. But his obviously modest circumstances precluded that, and he had postponed it indefinitely.

The second presentation ended. Mr Rane answered various questions about earnings expectations for the following quarter, and then invited the audience to lunch. Vishwas waited for the others to drift away before he made his way to the finance director.

'Sir, I am Vishwas, a freelance journalist. I have a small question. There were a few photographs of a village school in the first presentation. Can you tell me the name of the village?'

'I presume you mean the slides on corporate social responsibility. I'm afraid I am the finance man, you will have to ask Shash herself.'

'Has she left?'

'Probably yes. She has another important meeting this afternoon.'

'It's rather important for my story. Is there anyone else who would know?'

'I'm afraid not. Ms Dubey takes this social responsibility stuff rather seriously and runs the programme herself. I believe she personally took those photographs. I just account for the bills.'

'Is there some way I can contact her?'

'Why not give it a try? Let me give you her local number. As you can imagine, she is very busy but should be in town for the next two days.'

Vishwas took down the number on the notepad in his press kit. For once he did not join in the scramble for an extra corporate gift.

It was mid-afternoon by the time Vishwas finished eating the post-event lunch and walked out to the promenade. He felt strangely unsettled by the rekindling of suppressed memories. He felt alone amid all the bustle that greeted him on the street. Perhaps the art gallery would calm him. He had intended to visit it anyway. He always preferred writing about art.

The Arder House Artists' Gallery (Established 1950) was a short walk from the hotel. The gallery was largely empty. The paintings, in acrylic and oil, showed monks of an indeterminate eastern denomination engaged in various meditations. A write-up about the artist had been hung next to the entrance. It read:

> Daabvala's paintings of this period are often about the renouncer. It is a body that makes imperious claims, ringing through the confident stance of the feet, the poise of carriage and the nobility of the domed head . . .

Vishwas would normally have copied all this down, and then reflected on each painting in turn. Today, however, the paintings of multicoloured monks offered no relief. It all seemed awkward, complicated and distant. He left the gallery and wandered the streets trying to clear his head. He walked through the bazaar, past shops and eateries, past the offices of stockbrokers and banks. He lingered again at the second-hand bookstalls at Fountain before taking the train to Charni Road. A head massage at dusk on Chowpatty Beach provided temporary relief. He then treated himself to a dinner of paneer bhurji and butter-roti at Crystal. It was past rush hour by the time he walked back to the train station and headed home. He spent the evening alone, immersed in rum, Rafi and Vikram Sampath's book on Gauhar Jaan.

The next morning, Vishwas called Ms Dubey's office. She was in a meeting but he left his name and his query with the secretary, and was asked to call back. A few hours later, he called back.

'Ma'am, this is Vishwas. I had called a few hours ago. Did you manage to convey my query to Ms Dubey?'

'Oh yes. She would like to meet you. Can you come to our office tomorrow at noon? It's on the fourth floor of Maker Chambers VI, Nariman Point. Do you know how to get here?'

'Yes, I know where it is.'

'See you tomorrow, then. Please be on time, she has to catch a flight soon after your interview.'

Vishwas was somewhat taken aback to be invited for a personal interview. Perhaps they had mistaken him for a journalist from a major publication. It did not matter, he now had an opportunity to meet the lady herself—a stroke of luck.

He woke up earlier than usual the next day. After getting himself a 'special shave' at Gokul Haircutting Saloon down the street, he put on his best shirt before heading for the station. He arrived at the office with several minutes to spare and, after a short wait, was shown into the CEO's office. She sat behind a large desk and greeted him with a radiant smile.

'Ah, my hunch was right. You are the same Vishwas I knew in my childhood. It's a pleasure to meet you after so long. You have changed, but I can still recognize you.'

'You know me from childhood?'

'Of course. We are both from Kausambi. I thought you knew.'

'So those photos are indeed of Kausambi.'

'And you knew me as a girl. My father was the headmaster. Surely you remember him.'

Vishwas was stunned.

'Yes—I now remember. You are Shashwati!'

'I used to watch you play cricket with the other boys. Then, you went away to university and never returned. But I never forgot you. I used to overhear our fathers discuss you. Then, in my final year at high school, your father gave me a box with many of your books. Premchand, Narayan, Borges, Tagore, Manto, Steinbeck, Orwell . . . I read them all . . . and all your detailed notes on the margins and on scraps of paper.'

'So it was you who inherited those books!'

'Yes. I really enjoyed them and your commentaries. I am quite grateful to you as they opened my mind to a wider world. I am sure I still have all of them stored somewhere. We had barely ever spoken to each other before now, but there was a time when, through your scribbled notes, I knew you better than anyone else in the world. Sitting in Kausambi, I dreamed of distant lands . . .

Perhaps it's easier now with satellite television and mobile phones . . .'

'I cannot believe this! I had no idea! How did you become such a big businesswoman?'

'About fourteen years ago, I married a lawyer when I was still at university. He is a successful advocate at Allahabad High Court. I started a small business largely to entertain myself but it did very well. My father-in-law and a cousin lent me money to expand the business. I have not looked back since.'

'I suppose you return regularly to Kausambi for the school project. Are your parents still there?'

'I do occasionally visit the village project but it is usually hurried. My father passed away six years ago. My mother now lives with us—she looks after the kids since I have to travel so much. Enough about me. Tell me, what have you been up to?'

Over a cup of tea, Vishwas gave her a brief outline. They were interrupted by a knock on the door.

'Ma'am, the car is waiting.'

'Vishwas, I have to rush now. Got a flight to catch. It was a pleasure to catch up with you after so long. Please leave your contact details with my secretary and perhaps we can meet for coffee when I am here next . . . possibly next month. See you.'

Vishwas watched her pick up her laptop bag and rush out of the door. He stared out of the window at the blue–grey of the sea, the cluster of tall skyscrapers across the inlet and the dark clouds in the far horizon that promised the onset of monsoon rains. At least he now knew where his first collection of books had ended up. Perhaps he could manage to persuade her to return them.

Exile

In the evening
When the temple bells ring
We remember
The lands we left behind

    The stars were brighter
    The snow was whiter
    The peaches sweeter
    The restless river

In the evening
When the monsoon winds blow
We remember
The lands we left behind

    The fields were greener
    The birds sang sweeter
    The peaks rose higher
    The moon shone brighter

In the evening
When the fireflies glow
We remember
The lands we left behind

> *The streams were clearer*
> *The girls prettier*
> *Their smiles brighter*
> *Our burdens lighter*

In the evening
When the little ones sleep
We wonder
About the lands we left behind

> *Who tends my garden?*
> *Who smells my roses?*
> *Who reads my papers?*
> *Who rides my horses?*

And does anyone still sing hymns to the sun?

A Revolution in Humours

A long time ago, in the City where the Three Rivers meet, the greatest medical minds of the East gathered for the Grand Council. The Grand Council was held every ten years. The king invited philosophers, physicians, surgeons, alchemists and healers. For nine nights and ten days they discussed the latest advances in surgical technique, swapped remedies, debated the secrets of longevity and boasted about the miraculous healings of the previous decade. Elixirs and potions were proposed and debated.

Many others too flocked to the Grand Council—nobles and princes, merchants and lay citizens, priests and astrologers. They listened with fascination and awe to the wisdom of all these learned men. Sometimes, a wondrous, novel remedy would find favour and, within weeks, come into use in lands far and wide. At other times, a surgeon or alchemist would offer a radical new idea that would make him a household name across the land. The Grand Council was an institution that had survived kings and dynasties, wars and famines. The events recounted in this tale relate to the thirty-sixth and last Grand Council.

The thirty-sixth Grand Council was thrown open as usual by the king with an extravagant ceremony—dancing girls from the Yava Dwipa, acrobats from Cathay, bards from Champa, contortionists from Muziris, elephants from Taprobane and fantastic animals from the Land of Zanj. The City was alive with festivity. In other lands, such festivity would have been reserved for a royal coronation or for the Festival of the Moon, but here the citizens celebrated their love of knowledge and intellectual pursuit.

The inns and taverns were bursting full. A city of tents had been erected outside the walls of the City to accommodate the visitors. Some of the better-known doctors, philosophers and medical schools had their own special enclosure where their entourage could stay together. In the fairgrounds, merchants assembled to sell herbs, potions and miracle cures from distant lands. A clutch of holy men showed off their mental control by walking on burning coal and sleeping on nails.

It was during the inaugural feast that evening that news spread of the arrival of a legendary physician from beyond the Western Seas. His name was Maraksh. Little was definitively known about him in these parts but foreign merchants and travellers had spread his fame and stature. It was, therefore, not surprising that the news was universally acclaimed. The king was especially pleased at the opportunity to host such a venerated guest. Future generations would remember his reign by this occasion.

The next morning, a flotilla of boats rowed up the river. Their oars dipped and rose in unison to the slow, regular beat of drums. Their bright red flags fluttered in the breeze. The boats dropped anchor below the palace walls. A messenger soon appeared before the royal assembly announcing the arrival of the great physician Maraksh and his entourage. They had crossed deserts, oceans and rivers to come and attend the Grand Council, and requested permission to set foot on land. The king offered the exalted guest and his followers a grand welcome, and gave orders for the necessary arrangements to be made for their stay. The southern wing of the palace was opened up specially for the famed physician and his party.

That afternoon, after the midday meal, the Grand Council witnessed the arrival of a legend. The entourage numbered over a hundred—servants, scribes, alchemists— all in flowing robes of red, the colour of blood. Only Maraksh himself was in a robe of spotless white. Flowing white beard, flowing white locks and eyes that blazed. And from his neck hung an enormous red ruby.

All those present were dazzled by the display and the royal demeanour. Maraksh walked on to the dais, bowed once to the king, and then took his place without a word. For the rest of the afternoon, he listened patiently as distinguished scholars put forward their thoughts and findings of the previous decade. Maraksh asked no questions, he offered no opinions. He did not speak on the following day either, when the chief royal physician gave a discourse on the principal causes of melancholy and its appropriate cures. He said nothing even when the scholars of Cipangu hotly contested the Yavan view on the medical importance of flatulence.

Yet, even in his silence, Maraksh had no dearth of admirers. More and more citizens now crowded into the assembly hall for a glimpse of this remarkable man and his followers. They whispered amongst themselves and waited. There was an air of expectation.

Then, at last, on the fourth day, Maraksh rose to speak. There was a hushed silence. His voice was powerful yet measured, deep yet cutting. His eyes blazed as he spoke. He first thanked the king and the citizens for their hospitality. He said it was a great honour to address such a distinguished gathering.

Then, to a stunned audience, he proceeded to propound a medical philosophy that would destroy the very foundations of the science as it was known in the East.

He said that the learned men who had gathered at the council were right to say that the maladies of body and mind were due to imbalances between their constituent humours. The goal of all medical remedies is to restore equilibrium between these humours. So far so good. However, he disagreed with virtually everything else. Most importantly, he was shocked and anguished that the learned physicians of the East were only aware of three humours when the ancient philosophers of Ionia had established beyond doubt that there were five. For were there not five elements in nature—water, earth, fire, air and the void? Were there not five senses, five planets, five fingers on each hand? It was clear that the number five was the organizing principle of the universe. So there must indeed be five humours in everyone:

- *Blood* that was hot and sweet, and resided in the head and the veins
- *Phlegm* that was cold and moist, and resided in the lungs
- *Choler* that was dry, hot and bitter, and resided in the gall bladder
- *Black bile* that was sour and cold, and resided in the spleen
- *Pneuma* that was dry and cold but without taste, and resided in the heart

The failure to recognize the second and fourth humours meant that all existing systems of Eastern diagnosis were fundamentally flawed and needed to be replaced. Melancholy, for instance, was not caused by an imbalance between blood and choler as supposed by the chief royal physician but by the excess of pneuma and black bile. The combination of these excess humours caused malodorous fumes to rise to the head and affected the blood therein. Sweating, the application of hot cups and eating of warm foods, therefore, brought no benefits to those suffering from melancholy. Instead, they must be treated with small quantities of mercury and the herb hellebore. The use of leeches on the neck was also recommended in the more severe cases in order to remove bad blood from the head. The breathing of smoke from dried horse dung clearly helped counteract the malodorous fumes and should be administered three times a day after meals.

Maraksh then went on to expound on the key methods of diagnosis using the new methodology. By the time he finished outlining the broad principles, it was past midnight but not a single person in the audience had stirred, their minds dazzled by new ideas. However, not everyone was pleased. The established members of the Physicians Guild were furious at having their long-held practices publicly debunked and ridiculed. They lobbied with the king to bar the foreigner from speaking further and to expunge his name from all records.

The chief royal physician even expressed his suspicion that the man was not the real Maraksh but an imposter. But the younger physicians and surgeons rallied to support the foreigner. They argued that change was inevitable and the presentation of new ideas was in the spirit of the Grand Council. The citizenry and the younger members of the nobility agreed. The king sensed the popular mood. Besides, he himself was intrigued by the possibilities offered by the new philosophical framework. He deferred the other speakers and urged Maraksh to continue the next day.

When the speaker and his entourage returned the next morning, they found the hall of assembly even more crowded than before. Overnight, the news of revolution had spread and people from nearby villages and towns had flocked to the City to hear the seer speak. Some had even climbed up nearby trees to get a better view. Maraksh argued that the study of medical conditions required an improved system of classification. He then expounded on a scientific taxonomy that had first been proposed by Diophanes, the chosen disciple of the legendary Al-Flatun. According to Diophanes, all maladies and afflictions should be classified as follows:

- Colds and aches accompanied by fever
- Typhus
- Consumption
- Maladies that affect the left-handed
- Flukes, fleas and other parasites
- Melancholy
- Rage

- Injuries sustained in battle
- Injuries sustained on Sundays
- Plagues and poxes
- Maladies caused by bad air
- Maladies caused by the surfeit of blood
- Maladies that affect sailors
- Poisons

Maraksh explained in brief the major symptoms of each group of conditions, and the humoral imbalances that caused them. He elaborated on Hirophilos' doctrine on the pulse. Maraksh explained that he agreed that the tremors of the heart mirrored imbalances of the system but it was important to understand the musical theories of Aristoxenus of Tarentum in order to read them.

The next day, the seer put forward a detailed exposition of the various techniques and treatments that were available to the practised physician to restore the five humours to equilibrium. These included diets and potions, baths and massages, bloodletting, purges, emetics, sweating and the application of hot cups. For poisons, the antidotes of Abu Musa Jabir were especially recommended. Surgery was an option with certain problems although opinion was still divided on its effectiveness in treating conditions other than the loss of blood.

There were numerous ways in which roots, herbs, bones and minerals could be combined to produce potions.

Philosophers had devised elaborate taxonomies for the scientific classification of ingredients. According to Maraksh, however, the only sensible way to classify herbs was thus:

- Herbs that did not have green leaves
- Herbs that thrived in winter
- Herbs that came from foreign lands to the south
- Herbs that came from foreign lands to the east
- Herbs that grew in the king's garden
- Herbs that tasted sour
- Herbs that tasted bitter after being treated with sulphur
- The seven herbs mentioned by Ibn-Nadir in his treatise on snakebites
- Mushrooms

By now, reports of the new prophet of medicine had made their way to the more distant towns and villages, and even to neighbouring kingdoms. Citizens, merchants, princes and even peasants flocked to the City where the Three Rivers meet. Some of the merchants in the fairground had already changed their potions to reflect the new system. Some of them, now dressed in robes of red, even claimed to have personally known Maraksh in their travels across the Western seas.

Meanwhile, in the assembly hall, the royal scribes worked furiously to record the words of wisdom. But the established physicians were not willing to give in so easily to the usurper. The grand master of the Physicians Guild rose to speak.

'We are grateful, O Maraksh, for the many novel ideas that you have presented before us in these few days. We will all agree that you have been most entertaining. However, you must demonstrate the efficacy of your methods. Your novel prescriptions must now be put to the test for all to see.'

The king agreed that this was indeed a reasonable request. So he asked the Royal Council of Physicians to put forward a suitable test. After some deliberation, it was decided to produce the kingdom's most famous patient— the king's elder brother. Sometime in his youth, the prince's mind had become afflicted by rage. He swore at all around him and had to be restrained from doing bodily harm to others. The old king, his father, had invited physicians, healers, astrologers and magicians from lands far and near but they had all failed to find a cure. Indeed, the affliction worsened with time. At last, the crown prince had to be locked away in a tower in the castle and his younger brother, the present king, was placed as next in the line of succession. The former crown prince had not been seen in public for many years but, sometimes late at night, the citizens heard screams that were neither human nor animal.

The prince was summoned to the assembly hall the next day. His appearance was fearsome. Clothes in tatters, his long beard and hair tangled and knotted, a wild fury in his eyes. He swore at the crowds, at the nobles, at the king. But for the chains and shackles, he would have lunged at anyone nearby.

Maraksh examined him from a distance, slowly walking in a circle around him. Gravely he consulted the Papyrus of Imhotep. Then he asked his alchemists to prepare a potion of equal parts of mercury, the fat of a serpent born on a full moon and the paste of the Paxillus mushroom. This mixture was force-fed to the prince every two hours, along with red wine. All other food was forbidden. The prince showed no signs of improvement on the first day, nor on the second. Maraksh asked for patience.

Then, on the third day, the prince reappeared, accompanied by the alchemists in red. Everyone was astonished at the transformation. The chains and shackles had been removed. He was clean-shaven, his hair was tidy and he wore new royal robes. His steps faltered a little and he had to be supported by a retainer, but he appeared collected. The wild fire in his eyes had been extinguished. He was led to a seat beside the king where he sat calmly, not speaking a word. His face had an angelic serenity, his eyes fixed in the distance.

No one was in doubt that Maraksh had performed a miracle. This was proof of the power of the new system. The audience cheered wildly—citizens, nobles, merchants and peasants. The established physicians were forced to accept defeat.

Maraksh now requested permission to take his leave. The king gifted him three chests of silver and four of gold. He begged the seer to return. Maraksh then led his entourage back to the boats and the flotilla rowed down the river from whence it had come. That night, the former crown prince died peacefully in his sleep.

Soon there were rumours that the court physicians had poisoned the prince to avenge their humiliation and to discredit the philosophy of five humours. The king was not especially bereaved. Indeed, the recovery of his elder brother, the former crown prince, had raised some uncomfortable possibilities. But he knew that justice must be seen to have been done. The chief royal physician and the grand master were arrested and charged with murder, treason and conspiracy. They confessed their guilt after a week of torture and were sentenced to death. Their bodies were impaled at the city gates as an example to all.

With the blessings of the palace, a group of young physicians and nobles proceeded to purge the medical fraternity. The old texts and manuals were forcibly confiscated and burned publicly. The guilds were reformed and cleansed. All mention of the old system of three humours was banned under a law aimed at eradicating superstition. Every physician and surgeon was sent back to be re-educated in the new rational and progressive methods. Those who refused were imprisoned and sent away to work in the salt mines.

The old ideas are no longer to be found in the Land of the Three Rivers, except perhaps in some remote mountain hamlet. Many kings and dynasties have come and gone, but a bronze statue of Maraksh still stands tall in the city bazaar. However, the Grand Council is no longer held every ten years. Soon after the thirty-sixth council, the new incumbents of the medical fraternity decided to discontinue it on the grounds that it encouraged dangerous new ideas.

Drivers

Till the end of the twentieth century, Siberian cranes used to fly to India every winter. These birds no longer come, perhaps extinct. They have been replaced by a new kind of winter migration: Indians working in Western think tanks and American universities, who descend on major Indian cities, especially Delhi, between the second week of December and the third week of January. A few stragglers stay back till the end of the month to attend literature festivals. Then, as suddenly as they have appeared, they fly back to their nesting grounds in Boston, New York, Washington DC, Geneva, London and so on.

All migrating species have their favourite watering holes to sustain them over the season. Just as the Rann of Kutch comes alive with the flamingoes in winter, so it is with the 'golden triangle' of real estate between India International Centre, Khan Market and Taj Palace hotel—seminars, conferences, book readings, political gossip, cocktail parties, hobnobbing in general. A few foraging parties may make their way to shop in Connaught Place, perhaps a round or two at Delhi Golf Club, meetings on Raisina Hill. Thus, over coffee and single malts they hammer out what a senior journalist has dubbed as the 'Khan Market Consensus' on how to improve India and Indians.

Hardeep 'Hardy' Singh reached out for the menu even though he should have known it almost by heart by now. He had been here three times in the past three days, catching up with different groups of friends and acquaintances. Tortoise Cafe is on the second floor, just above a bookshop by the same name. It is small and crowded but popular with everyone in the set. So, one only needed to spend an afternoon or two there to catch up with all the gossip.

Hardy glanced through the menu quickly, then ordered his usual coffee and brownie. His companion, Anil Ahuja, ordered tea and cheesecake. They had grown up in the Delhi of the seventies and early eighties and had known each other all their lives: Panchsheel Enclave, Modern School, Delhi University's North Campus, then together to the US for postgraduate studies. Anil had even dated Hardy's sister briefly although that had not ended well. Hardy was now the South Asia expert at a policy think tank in Washington DC; Anil was the Peter J. Hull Professor of Development Studies at the University of New Haven.

'So, how's it going?'

'Busy, very busy. Got a bunch of stuff going on. Have to pull together this paper for a conference in Chicago in Feb. We have all this great RCT data from Kenya and my RAs need to finish crunching the numbers over Christmas. Then I need to get back to my publishers on my next book on the impact of primary health interventions in developing countries. By the way, I have a great foreword from Joe.'

'Are you making it to Jaipur for the Lit Fest?'

'Not likely. Have to drop by Davos. Yet again the dates clash. Cannot understand why the Jaipur chaps do not understand how inconvenient it is.'

'Hope you remember my event in DC—it's April 28th. No excuses.'

'Have blocked the dates . . . Ah, there is Penny . . . and John!'

Penny Atwood was the South Asia bureau chief of a leading American newspaper. Both Hardy and Anil wrote occasional columns for her. John Anderson was a former journalist who had spent more than a decade in Delhi and was now the resident 'old India hand' for various British establishments. He had also written books about the 'real India' of sadhus, monkeys and poverty. These books were considered required reading by newly arrived Western aid workers and were widely quoted in their brochures. Everyone in Khan Market knew John.

'Sorry for being late . . . the traffic is awful. We were stuck near AIIMS for ages.'

'Tea or coffee?'

'Probably shouldn't have any more coffee today. Maybe a juice or something . . .'

'How is Delhi treating you?'

'But for the pollution, it's tolerable this time of year. Must make sure I go back to New York for peak summer next year.'

'Come down to DC, we'll take you out for a full tour of the bars in Georgetown.'

'Why don't I ever get the full tour of Georgetown?'

'Ha ha ha. It's only Dupont Circle for you . . .'

'. . . and Founding Farmers!'

'Perhaps we should get Founding Farmers to set up a branch at the IMF office in Delhi.'

'The key to surviving Delhi, as I have learned, is a good cook, a good driver and Mussoorie.'

'Speaking of drivers, my driver just told me that the UP elections will be close . . . He's from some place near Varanasi . . . Mirzapur . . .'

'Great place to buy carpets, I'm told.'

'Are you planning a trip to see some of the campaigning? It will peak in the next two weeks.'

'Can't see how I can get away from Delhi with all the stuff going on. And John suggested a great story about the monkey problem on Raisina Hill. Such a great idea!

Should be able to get a full spread in the weekend supplement.'

'I hope you get some interesting photos to go with it.'

'Oh yes, that goes without saying. Do we need official permission to photograph on Raisina Hill?'

'Not sure, but I'm sure we can talk to somebody and arrange it if necessary.'

'Hey, isn't that Baby John?'

Professor B. John was emerging up the narrow stairwell into the cafe accompanied by a couple. Early fifties, Einsteinesque moustache, oily hair, khaki chinos and the loose corduroy jacket loved by academics the world over. His parents had lovingly named him Baby, which had been tolerable when he was two, but became the source of endless smirking later in life. Not surprisingly, he had changed it to the more grandiose Balthazar when he had taken up US citizenship. He strongly resented people from the old days, therefore, who remembered the old name and insisted on using it.

'Hardy, Anil, what a pleasant surprise . . . Haven't seen the two of you since Geneva . . . How long are you in Delhi?'

'Hi, I am Penny.'

'John Anderson . . . pleased to meet you.'

'Pleased to meet you too, I am Balthazar.'

'Oh, didn't realize you did not know each other. Balthazar is associate professor at Rhode Island State.'

'And let me introduce my sister, Lily, and brother-in-law, Vijayan. They live in Delhi. Vijayan is a civil servant, Lily teaches at DPS.'

'Come join us. Pull up a couple of chairs . . . and that table. Should we order a pot of tea?'

'Yes, that would be great.'

The newly arrived took their seats. Vijayan was a short, slim man but for a small paunch; his bald patch was barely covered by a comb-over, his coat a size too big. His official identity card dangled loosely from a blue strap around his neck.

'How long are you in Delhi this winter?'

'Maybe two weeks . . . Have this workshop in JNU and the usual catching up with friends. Would have stayed longer but have to visit my folks in Cochin for a week. By the way, I have this invitation to do a lecture at Ashoka— how long does it take to their campus?'

'Depends on where you are staying . . .'

'With Lily and Vijayan in Netaji Nagar.'

'It will take you at least ninety minutes each way from IIC.'

'Yeah, it uses up half a day. That's if the traffic is good.'

'Really, the traffic gets worse every year.'

'You remember that report I compiled two years ago on a Comprehensive Urban Transport Plan for India? Had some great papers from the Barcelona workshop. No action. I even sent a copy to the transport minister.'

'I know what you mean. I have been talking about the dengue situation for the last four years. Even had a paper on it in the *International Journal of Health Economics*. No action. Do they even know how difficult it is to publish in *IJHE*?'

'No one reads quality journals in India.'

'I published a brief, nontechnical version for Penny. At least they should have read that.'

'The country has been taken over by the riffraff mofussil types—they don't read. They will rant on Twitter, listen to more ranting on television and spend the rest of their time walking up and down shopping malls.'

'That's why I really avoid the malls, especially the ones in Gurgaon.'

'Why on earth do you even go to Gurgaon?'

'My publishers have their office there—needed to meet my editor. Never again. Next time I will ask her to come here.'

'So, what is the next project?'

'Thinking of writing an article on the impact of the JDY scheme on the poor.'

'Total failure, if you ask me.'

'Such a colossal waste, I tell you.'

'I am no expert, but I am told that it has been a big success in rural areas and even with the urban poor.'

This was the first time Vijayan had participated in the conversation. He had been quietly sitting next to his brother-in-law and sipping tea. Now everyone turned to look at him. He continued, 'There was a positive article about it in the *Economic Times* this morning. Also, one of my batchmates runs JDY in Rajasthan. He was mentioning that it was working well. But, as I said, I am no expert.'

'You cannot believe Indian news reports. These reporters don't understand anything. I took this taxi from the airport yesterday and the driver told me that JDY did not help him at all.'

'Yeah, my parents' cook, been with us for decades, was telling me that his sister tried to use JDY back in the village. Didn't work.'

'It's not really my department. I just know what I hear from others.'

'You government babus should really talk to people at the grass roots, you know. That's the only way to find out what's really going on.'

'Yeah, you should at least talk to your driver . . .'

Expatriate Indians and foreign journalists have long nurtured the belief that their drivers are the best source of information on the mysterious workings of the country. The drivers, of course, know this and have learned that the best tips are elicited by simply reinforcing each person's existing beliefs. Waiting outside for their employers to finish their long dinners, they huddle together and exchange gossip on what works best on the ego of each employer.

It was a working day, so Vijayan left Lily and Balthazar to carry on with the conversation and went back to office. He mildly resented the trips to Tortoise Cafe with Balthazar every winter, but Lily insisted on it. She argued that Balthazar was doing them a favour by introducing them to the right sort of people and Vijayan should really learn to make friends with them. He had tried his best but as the sole representative of the government at these gatherings, he felt that the others held him personally responsible for every lapse of governance. This was particularly unfair since the mid-level bureaucrat was frankly in no position to change the way the country was run.

For the last five years, O.P. Vijayan had been posted to the Organizing Committee of the Delhi Asian Games 1982. Three and a half decades had passed since the event but there had been several unresolved issues, ranging from financial accounts to legal disputes, that had kept the body from being shut down. Now the committee consisted only of Vijayan, an assistant and a pile of old files. The officer had slowly worked his way through the files and resolved most of the issues, but one last case was stuck in the Supreme Court, one of 33 million cases stuck in the judicial system. Hence, the Organizing Committee of the Delhi Asian Games could not be wound up and Vijayan worried that the rest of the government had forgotten him.

This was not an idle concern as Vijayan's office was in a building that was known as the graveyard of many a civil servant's career. The building had been built in the early seventies when Socialist Brutalism was the height of fashion. The architect, who was incidentally the public works minister's son-in-law, had won an award for it. The concrete exterior was uniformly grey except for the motley signboards of government offices and the streaks of green algae that oozed from leaking pipes. This was where dead-end public projects and obscure departments were sent to live out their days.

Vijayan walked down the corridor to the back of the building. Lined along the corridor were rusting iron frames stacked with dusty files that had not been consulted for years, perhaps decades. The office of the Organizing Committee of the Delhi Asian Games 1982 was on the second floor. Vijayan was not surprised to find that the lift was still not working, and walked up the narrow stairs. All along were signs prohibiting spitting but generations of tobacco chewers had disdainfully expressed their dissent in every corner.

Vijayan's cabin had been carved out of a larger room with the help of floor-to-ceiling aluminium partitions. Inside, there was a steel-frame shelf for files, a green–grey Godrej almirah, a desk and an office chair with the obligatory pale-blue towel draped over it. The partition had left the cabin without windows so that the only source of air circulation was an old air conditioner that rattled constantly and dripped into a small bucket. Numerous requests had been made for a replacement but the funds had not been sanctioned.

Mercifully the cabin was tolerable without air conditioning for a couple of months in winter. The room was silent that afternoon, therefore, when Vijayan leaned back on his towel-draped chair and contemplated his life—the decades of bureaucratic drudgery. Perhaps he should have joined the private sector, or followed his heart and become a writer, or followed Balthazar to America. Instead, here he was, sitting in a windowless cabin, fighting a legal battle for a committee that should have been wound up before he had even started his career.

He stared at the pile of papers pertaining to the last remaining case and wondered why he had never tried to break out of the drudgery. Maybe it was inertia. Maybe he had held out hope that a career in the civil services would eventually yield to more meaningful responsibilities. But it was too late now to start over. He just had to keep going till he retired. With these thoughts floating through his mind, he pulled the case files towards himself and began to read them afresh.

Like many Indians, Vijayan had inherited a legal dispute that had been handed down through several generations like a prized heirloom. A couple of months earlier, he had managed to win the decades-old case.

It did not yield much by way of financial gain but was seen by his family as a moral victory against a distant branch of the clan. Now, as he reread the files of the Asian Games, Vijayan wondered if he could somehow win the last case.

The civil servant threw himself into the case. Perhaps it was an attempt to reclaim the last vestiges of self-worth. Lily had certainly never seen him this energized. He followed up with government lawyers, hunted down fine legal details and pushed for an early hearing. The legal tussle had made its way through the lower courts, through the high court to the Supreme Court where it had languished from apathy. No one expected a quick resolution. Vijayan's energetic advocacy, however, yielded a fresh hearing within a few weeks . . . and the new approach worked! A three-judge bench ruled unanimously in favour of the government. Since this was a judgment of the apex court, there was no appeal. The Organizing Committee of the Delhi Asian Games 1982 could be wound up at last.

~

The Supreme Court ruling on the final Delhi Asian Games case coincided with a major scandal that engulfed senior bureaucrats in the central government. An internal investigation had revealed widespread criminal negligence and corruption. A systematic pattern of collusion and nepotism had perpetuated the system for years and the investigation reports were damning. Several senior civil servants were forced to resign overnight. The prime minister ordered the transfer of several others. Additional investigations were ordered.

The prime minister slowly flipped through the Sunday newspapers. He sipped his tea and turned the pages. The headlines were dominated by the scandal. The opinion pages were divided between those who praised the political leadership for finally taking on large-scale corruption in the bureaucracy and others who criticized the prime minister for tolerating such a crooked cabal for so long.

The spate of resignations and transfers had created a big vacuum in the higher bureaucracy. It was not a tenable situation. The prime minister's first priority was to find replacements as soon as possible. The matter was on top of his mind when he came across an article tucked away on the ninth page. It was a report on how the Organizing Committee of the Delhi Asian Games 1982 had finally been wound up. It also told of an official, O.P. Vijayan, who had worked diligently for five years to complete the financial accounts of the committee and had gone on to win the last legal battle. The report further described the intricacies of the case.

The prime minister picked up the phone and asked his private secretary to come in. He then requested for more information about the officer mentioned in the article. A month later, Vijayan was appointed as director general of Foreign Trade. He was given a large office in Udyog Bhavan with a generous view of Raisina Hill. His family moved into one of the semi-detached houses in Pandara Park. Lily was very pleased to have her own garden. She was equally pleased that she was now within walking distance of Khan Market. She could now engage with her brother's friends on more equal terms.

Vijayan took to his new job like a duck to water. He had never had much interest in exports and imports, but the sudden elevation re-energized him. He quickly familiarized himself with the intricacies of free trade agreements and non-tariff barriers. Colleagues, some of whom had been in the ministry for years, were impressed by his ability to pick out the relevant details and offer innovative solutions to complex issues.

It had been less than a year in the new role for Vijayan when he received an invitation to speak at an important conference on trade and globalization in Washington DC. Lily was very excited and proud. She convinced Balthazar to fly down from Rhode Island for the event. He told her that Hardy and Anil Ahuja were almost certainly going to attend.

But Vijayan felt a bit nervous. This was the first time he had been asked to address such an important international gathering. He worked hard on his speech.

Facts and figures were checked and rechecked. The flow of arguments was meticulously worked out. Still, when Vijayan boarded the flight, he was not entirely satisfied. The body of the speech was good but he needed a simple, easy way to begin. He wracked his brain on the long flight for a chatty opening line. All the suggestions from his department sounded like formal officialese.

The event was held in the large ballroom of a prominent hotel. Vijayan sat on the dais, looking smart in his new *bandhgala*, tailor-made at Mohanlal's. Looking up from his notes at the large audience gathered in front of him, he thought he could discern Balthazar, Anil and Hardy sitting together in the dark somewhere at the back.

Vijayan walked confidently to the podium when the moderator invited him to speak.

'Secretary General Edward Kwabena, Deputy Secretary Susan Harman, Senator John Hill, Ambassador Lee, ladies and gentlemen. The debate over international trade and globalization has become a debate about inequality—inequality both within and between countries. The issue was brought into sharp focus when I was talking to the driver, a first-generation immigrant, who drove me in yesterday from the airport . . .'

The Return of Imagination

For twenty-five years I have travelled through all the lands marked in Ortelius' *Mappa Mundi*, and more. In the previous five volumes I have told of all the wondrous lands that I have visited—their peoples, their kings, the animals, the vegetation. Here I will record the last of my wanderings, in Tamrapura, the land of my birth.

When the winds blow to the north, the country of Tamrapura lies six weeks' sailing from Serendip. The Arabs and Ionians had long traded with merchants of Tamrapura for the fine muslin that was once famous throughout the world. However, that is now a memory as the looms of Tamrapura have fallen silent and the Arabs now flock to the port of Khambat for their wares.

I left the land of my birth when I was still a small child, too young to have any real recollections. My memories are but a few old tunes, the smells of the feasts and a language that I had not spoken in my adult life. I hazily remember my parents hastily bundling their belongings and me into a boat on a cold winter dawn. We sailed upstream to where the Three Rivers meet. From there to the mountains of the Kalash and further still. Thus began my life as a wanderer. We never stayed at any place for more than a few months, with my father's many friends. We lived in palaces and in tents. It was in the Rome of the Ionians that my mother died when I was ten. For some reason, my father always nursed a suspicion that the Ionian doctors had poisoned her.

We then travelled further west to the Land of the Franks. There, when I was fifteen, my father died in a Cathar monastery where we had taken refuge from the cold. He suffered a high fever for several days. In his delirium he spoke haphazardly of many things, of Tamrapura, of books, of treason and exile, my mother, long-forgotten friends. As the fever rose, he grew increasingly agitated but one could not decipher what he was saying. His last words were, 'Remember, my son, the limits to knowledge lie in your imagination.'

These were the last words I heard spoken in the language of my forefathers. The last words till I stood that day on the sandy banks waiting for the boatman. Other than me, there was a merchant and his motley servants. As I waited and listened, the half-forgotten tongue came drifting back from the depths—a strange and warm sensation, like meeting a long-lost friend.

It was a small boat with a solitary boatman. The boat was soon crowded with people and goods, and I found myself in the middle with the merchant. I asked in faltering words what I needed to pay. The merchant smiled, 'One only pays when one leaves Tamra. You are clearly new here, tell me what brings you to my country.' I explained that I was a wanderer and that this was the last of my wanderings. The merchant was pleased, he offered me his hospitality. He seemed a generous man and I accepted immediately.

The sandy banks shone golden in the sun while the palms drooped in the humid stillness. The merchant's servants unloaded and carried my bags as we set off on foot for the city of Tamrapura. This was fortunate as it was a day's journey from the landing spot and there were no porters to be hired. On both sides of the road, paddy grew in flooded fields. Here and there were groups of peasants, bent over, working the earth. At midday we rested and then resumed our journey.

As we neared the city, we saw in the distance a large gathering of men, women and children. They were beating their gongs and singing. It was an occasion of great merriment. Garlands, feasting and the incessant beating of the gongs. As we drew close, I saw that they had in the middle a man gagged and bound. The crowd was jeering and throwing stones at him. Bleeding and covered in dirt, he was a wretched sight. There was absolute terror in his eyes. I was somewhat dismayed and turned to the merchant for an explanation.

'Poor fellow, he must have offered to repair the clocks. The Elders do this to all those who try. He will now be burned at the stake. Many people realize it is wrong but they do not interfere for fear that the mob will instead turn against them. It is perhaps best that a man is sacrificed, there will now be peace for a year.'

We entered the city.

It was at once apparent that it had once been a great city. The merchant pointed with pride at beautiful temples and mansions, gardens and markets, but they were all in a state of neglect. Trees now wound their roots up the spires and the gutters overflowed. The gardens were overrun with squatters' warrens that exuded a stench. The citizens seemed too caught up in the bustle to notice. I was tired and grateful when we reached the merchant's house near the seashore. The sea breeze was cool; I slept well that night.

The next day, the merchant's son took me to see the city. We walked past the old wharves that had once welcomed merchants from far and near. Now they lay empty but for a few fishermen. We wandered through crowded bazaars where customers haggled endlessly but never bought anything. A people still proud, but now in rags. I felt sad and disappointed. This was where I was born, a land that had forgiven itself.

After two hours, we reached the central square. It was the only part of the city with a semblance of grooming. In the north was a soaring white palace, the palace of the king. To the south, an equally large building of Gothic solidity. The library of the Great Martyr, the boy told me with pride. To the east, a large pavilion where the Council of the Elders met. To the west, a clock tower—the clock still stuck at the hour that the Great Martyr had been murdered. Who had murdered him? Why? Why did all the clocks stop? No one knew. But there had been rumours that he had been killed by his most ardent followers so that they could worship him and immortalize him.

That evening I told the merchant that I wanted to present myself to the king. It was my custom to meet the rulers in all the lands that I visited. They were always glad to hear about distant lands. They treated me generously and showered me with presents that I may speak well of them to other kings on my travels.

The merchant, however, said it would not be possible. After the death of the Great Martyr, it had been decided to elect the oldest man in Tamra as the king. He was led to the palace and never allowed to leave. No one but officials could meet the royal prisoner. They informed him of all the matters of state and then listened to his considerations. However, they never carried out his orders. Instead, the scribes noted down every word and action. Only on the death of the king did his word become law. And so it remained till the death of the next king. The Elders and the people had deemed that this was the best way to ensure that no king would ever outshine the Great Martyr. I was amazed. In all these years of wandering, I had never seen or heard of such a custom.

The merchant sensed my disappointment at not being able to meet the king and, ever the good host, he proposed an alternative. 'Go and see the library—it is said to contain all the knowledge of the world. One of the Elders is my friend, I am sure he will agree to show you.' I was indeed pleased. I had overheard my father mentioning the library many times. It was the only thing about Tamrapura that I had heard him discuss with genuine pride.

A few days later, a man with a flowing white beard and a flowing white gown came to the merchant's house. He cut an impressive figure. He was Megha, the merchant's friend and one of the Elders. For the second time I visited the central square but this time we walked up the stairs into the library. Within its stone walls, it was cooler and darker. Megha led me into the central hall. There was a long wooden shelf with thick volumes bound in leather along one wall and wooden tables and benches along the other. A few scholars were deep in study. Even though it was day, it was so dark inside that they read by candlelight.

'The Great Martyr built this library. In it he compiled all the knowledge of the world.' He pointed to one end of the long shelf that held the thick volumes. Even in the dim light I could read the words written in gold: 'The Beginning of Knowledge'.

'There are 1008 volumes here. The first thousand contain all the knowledge collected by the Great Martyr from scholars from around the world—knowledge of philosophy, medicine, alchemy, astronomy, cartography, architecture. This hall was then full of debate and conjecture not seen since they burned down the Bibliotheca in Alexandria. The Great Martyr himself wrote the last eight volumes. They were his own contribution to thought. He was killed, mid-sentence, as he sat composing the last book. In his memory, no one is allowed to write another book.'

We had walked by now to the other end of the hall. Beyond the last eight volumes I discerned the words: 'The End of Knowledge'.

By the time we came out, afternoon had turned to dusk. I thanked the Elder and left. However, I did not walk back to the merchant's house but decided to amuse myself. I wandered the streets and marvelled at the grandeur of the old buildings. I wondered what had caused this once great civilization to decay. Walking aimlessly, I found myself back in the central square. It was dark now and deserted. Only a few lights shone from the palace windows. The prisoner-king who lived within intrigued me. No one appeared to be looking, and I decided to climb the clock tower in order to gain a vantage point over the palace walls.

The door to the clock tower was unlocked. I quietly crept up the spiral stairs and reached the top. The clock had stopped for over a century and made no sound. I opened one of the windows to look out over the palace courtyard. Inside, I could see a very old man by the flame of a torch. It was too far for me to discern his face, but he looked tired and lonely. Then, without even a whisper, I felt the cold edge of a sword at my neck. The palace guards bound me and dragged me down. They refused to answer any questions. I was thrown into a cold underground cell. I slept poorly that night, wondering what awaited me, hoping the merchant would find me and somehow get me out.

I was produced before the Council of Elders the next morning. Crowds of men, women and children surrounded the pavilion. They sang, they jeered and they beat their gongs, always the gongs. It had all the atmosphere of a festival except it was for my trial. The Elders sat in a semicircle, with their white robes and white beards. All glared sternly at me, including Megha who sat on the extreme left. Finally, one of them spoke.

'It is forbidden to look upon the king. All who dare must be burned at the stake.' The crowd cheered.

I replied that I was a foreigner who did not know the customs of Tamrapura. I had broken the rules through ignorance and not ill intent. I was worthy of forgiveness and mercy.

'You lie. You are no foreigner. Are you not the son of Agastya, the one whom we banished? You come here with mischief in your heart. You tricked the merchant for his hospitality and then Megha so that he would show you the library. You must burn.'

'I am indeed the son of Agastya but swear that I knew neither of his banishment nor of his crimes.'

'You lie again. You will burn tomorrow.' The crowds cheered as I was led away to the dungeon.

The day and then the night passed slowly in the darkness of the dungeon. I wondered about the sins of my father. I remembered all the places that I had visited—the kingdoms of the Franks, the island of Swarnadvipa, and Al Waq-Waq, the Land of Darkness that even Ibn-Batuta had not dared traverse. I had been shipwrecked near Cipangu, kidnapped by bandits outside Samarkand, lost in the deserts of Libya, fought in pitched battles against the Teutonic knights and survived to tell the tale. After all that, here I was doomed to be burned to death by my own people for a crime I could not fathom. I could not sleep that night but sat in the dark awaiting my fate.

It must have been well after midnight when I heard footsteps on the stairs leading down to the dungeon. The figure held a candle. It was Megha.

'I did not realize that you are Agastya's son. Your father was my friend and teacher. I was very sad when he was banished. At least he was allowed to live. There were many who thought he should have been executed.'

'What had he done to deserve such a punishment?'

'He claimed that he could complete the Great Martyr's last book. He argued that there were more books to be written.'

'So I will now be killed to satisfy that old bloodlust.'

'Not if you listen to me. I have bribed the guards to let you escape. I have also arranged for a horse outside the city gates. You must reach the ferry by daybreak. Here is a purse of gold coins that you will need to pay the boatman. In return, I ask only one favour.'

'I am hardly in a position to refuse.'

'Then take with you this boy, my son.'

I soon found myself in the central plaza with a purse of gold coins and a boy of about fourteen. The boy knew the way. In the moonlight, the library looked even grimmer. We walked quickly past the main entrance towards the city gates. However, I had no intention of leaving immediately. I asked the boy to follow me to the rear of the library building. The boy was unwilling but he obeyed. We crept along the back trying to see if any of the windows had been left unlocked. Finally, I found one that I could pry open. We hauled ourselves up.

Inside, we fumbled in the dark till I found a candle and lit it. We were in the central hall, standing next to the wall of books. A few more moments and I found what I was looking for—the last book. I quickly flipped through to the page where the Great Martyr had stopped dead mid-sentence.

Author's Note

I do not know what readers will make of this collection of short stories, but for me it is special—my first attempt at publishing fiction. It will come as something of a surprise to those who have read my non-fiction writings over the years, that I started writing this book, in bits and pieces, a decade and a half ago. In fact, when I first reached out to publishers circa 2005, it was to publish this book. However, no one was too keen on it and I was persuaded to write non-fiction. I am not complaining—it sent me on a happy journey and I will probably remain primarily a non-fiction writer. Nonetheless, the idea of publishing my short stories remained and I kept adding to and updating the collection. Only four of my original set have found their way here, but I am pleased to finally get it out there.

There are a couple of reasons that I so wanted to publish this book. First, I have long felt that the art of short story writing needs to be revived. Till the middle of the twentieth century, it was the dominant form of fiction

writing and most well-known authors across the world
practised the art. However, by the 1970s, short fiction was
replaced by the novel. Those who were once avid readers
of short stories in magazines and other periodicals, I am
told, moved on to television serials. As a result, the market
dried up and short fiction became a poor cousin of the
longer format. But I am not so sure of this explanation.
Hence this experiment.

The second motivation was to revive the art of
satire. India has a long tradition of satire going back to
ancient times. While it survives here and there in a few
Indian languages (and in social media), it is no longer a
mainstream art form. I am a firm believer that no society
can thrive unless it can occasionally mock itself. Hence,
many of the stories in this collection, albeit not all, have an
element of satire. I would like to clarify, nevertheless, that
all the characters are fictional and any apparent similarity
is merely due to the fact that satire, by its very nature, is
based on a caricature of real-world social mores.

As all writers know, publishing a book is a team
sport. So, let me end by thanking all the people who
helped me get this to the finishing line. My editors at
Penguin—Meru, Richa, Manasi and Arpita—for their
many suggestions that sharpened the plots and tightened
the language. Jit and Devangana for the quirky artwork.
My old friend Mimi who believed, all those years ago,
that the original set was worth publishing and sent me

down this path. Mayuresh and Varun for reading through the early versions and providing valuable feedback. And finally, Smita for patiently listening to the first draft of every piece of prose and verse, including the ones that did not ultimately make it here.